A FA
in the WINDOW

HILDA STAHL

Accent Books™ is an imprint of David C. Cook Publishing Co.
David C. Cook Publishing Co., Elgin, Illinois 60120
David C. Cook Publishing Co., Weston, Ontario
Nova Distribution Ltd., Newton Abbot, England

A FACE IN THE WINDOW

Revised 1992

Cover design and illustration by Terry Julien
First Printing, 1986
Printed in the United States of America
96 95 94 93 92 7 6 5 4 3

Library of Congress Catalog Card Number 85-73456

ISBN 0-78140-511-4

CONTENTS

1

STRANGE INTRUDERS

Wren turned the key in the lock, then slowly slipped into Mrs. Wheeler's empty house. The hot, closed-in air almost choked her as she walked to her favorite rocker in the front room. The silence wrapped around her and soothed her slightly. With a ragged sigh she sank down in the low rocker. Her clothes clung damply to her slight body. The rocker creaked and a car honked outdoors. Tomorrow school started and she'd be in fifth grade. Tomorrow she'd have to see Tim Avery again.

She shook her head and her brown hair flipped around her narrow face and thin shoulders. Her newly trimmed bangs could not hide the brown eyes which were big and sad in her sun tanned face.

"Tim Avery," she muttered, wrinkling her pert nose. In fourth grade he'd hung around her, talking to her every chance he got, smiling at her even when he knew it made her mad. She could not go through fifth grade with Tim hanging around her. He was dirty and poor and nobody liked him. The only reason he was allowed in JCA was because someone paid his way. He sure couldn't afford to go to a private Christian school on his own. He probably wasn't even a Christian. His family wasn't, and he didn't act like he was either.

"That dumb Tim Avery!" Wren clenched her small fist and the house key bit into her hand. She opened her hand and stared at the key resting on her palm. Jordan Christian Academy was not big enough for both her and Tim Avery.

A fly buzzed at the wide front window. The smell seemed worse today than it had the last time she'd come into the empty house to get away from Mom and Dad, Neil and Philip, and even her best friend Bess. Maybe she should open the windows each day to let in fresh air so that when Mrs. Wheeler came home from the hospital it would smell nice.

Wren eased up from the chair. Tugging down her blue tee shirt, she took a step toward the side window that opened easily. As she did, a key grated in the lock of the front door and she froze, her brown eyes wide with sudden fright. Mrs. Wheeler had given Mom and Dad a key to the side door only. Who was coming in? It couldn't be Mrs. Wheeler. She had to stay in the hospital for a long time after her stroke. No one else had a key.

Trembling, Wren slipped quietly behind the heavy sofa. Dust tickled her nose and she held it to keep back a sneeze. Her heart raced and perspiration soaked her body. The door opened and she peeked around the end of the sofa to see a man and woman walk into the room, half carrying, half dragging a boy about eight years old. His face was pale and his blue eyes wide. His red striped tee shirt hung outside his jeans and looked too big on his slight body.

"I wanna go home!" he cried, his voice cracking.

"You are home," snapped the woman in a sharp voice that sent shivers up and down Wren's spine. "I hope nobody saw us come in! Did you notice, George?"

"I told you no one was around, Jan. Can't you take my word for nothing? Can't you trust me to do anything right?" The man called George twitched his shaggy mustache. He wore a black polo shirt and faded jeans.

"Let's get him to the bedroom." The woman pulled on the boy, making him cry out. Wren shrank back and bit her lower lip to keep from shouting.

"Don't jerk him so hard, Jan," the man said.

"Then come on! I want to get him to his room so we can get settled in here and have dinner. I hope the old lady left her kitchen full of food."

Wren held her breath as they walked out of the front room and down the hall to the bedrooms. She heard a door creak and the murmur of voices. What should she do? If she waited, they might find her. But if she dashed to the side door, they might catch her and demand to know why she was there. She had to take the chance. She crawled out and ran to the side door, her heart in her mouth. Quietly she opened the door and slipped outside. The warm wind quickly dried the sweat on her face. Her hand shook as she pushed her key into her jeans' pocket. Her legs almost collapsed as she ran to a tall bush to hide until she could decide what to do. Mrs. Wheeler had not told her or her family about giving the front door key to anyone. Who were those people? Why were they being so mean to the boy? Could they be . . . kidnappers?

Wren gasped and her eyes widened. Kidnappers! Was it possible? She shivered in the hot summer afternoon.

Across the yard she heard Neil call her in to dinner, but she couldn't answer this close to the Wheeler house. She watched Neil run through their yard into the Wheeler yard and into Bess's yard.

"Wren! Where are you? It's time to eat!" At thirteen Neil was short, still waiting for his growth spurt, but his voice was beginning to change and it cracked about once every sentence. Sometimes he talked just to hear it crack. She watched as he stopped outside the back door of the Talbot house, and called, "Bess, have you seen Wren?"

The back door opened and Bess stepped out with a wide smile. She had blonde hair and blue eyes and was wearing pink jeans and shirt. Wren knew how much Bess like Neil. Neil had to be the only person alive who didn't know Bess was madly in love with him.

"Hello, Neil," Wren heard Bess say.

"Bess, is Wren here? I can't find her."

"I saw her about an hour ago, but she said she was going home." Bess bent her knees a little so that she wouldn't tower over Neil. Wren knew Bess was waiting for Neil's growth spurt, too. "Do you want me to help you find her?"

Neil shook his head and pushed his hands deep into his jeans' pockets. "If you see her, send her home. Neil turned away and Wren leaned closer to the bush so he wouldn't spot her and demand to know why she hadn't answered him. She didn't want him to know that she was outside the Wheeler house—and that she'd been inside just moments before.

"Goodbye, Neil," Bess said in a voice that she used only for Neil.

He mumbled goodbye and ran back to his yard and into the house, slamming the back door behind him.

Bess sighed and walked back into her house.

Wren peeked toward the Wheeler place and waited for another look at the people inside. But no one moved and the door remained closed.

"Hiding from your shadow, Wren?"

She jumped, then glared as she saw Paula Gantz. "What I do is no business of yours, Paula."

Paula looked down her nose at Wren. "You think you're so big, Bird House!"

Wren narrowed her dark eyes and doubled her fists at her sides. She hated it when people made fun of her name. "Get out of my way, Paula. I have to go home for dinner." Wren tried to push past Paula, but Paula shoved her into the bushes.

"Don't you want to hear my news?"

Wren rubbed her arm where a branch had scratched her. "No!"

"Well, you're going to hear it anyway." Paula stood with her hands on hips and her slender shoulders back. Excitement darkened her eyes. "Tomorrow I will not be going to public school. I am going to Jordan Christian Academy. So there!"

Wren gasped and almost fell into the bush. Life was suddenly very rotten, very very rotten. "You're teasing me, aren't you? You want to make me lose my temper and punch you right in the nose, don't you?"

Paula pushed her fingers through her short brown hair and laughed. "I am going to JCA and I'm going to be in fifth grade—the same as you and Bess. I bet my grades will be better than yours. And I bet I'll be asked to sing in all the school programs instead of you."

Wren pushed past Paula and ran to her back door, her head buzzing. She would not let Paula make her angry! Paula's parents would never permit her to attend a Christian school. Paula was lying, as usual. Wren stepped inside her back door. What if Paula was telling the truth?

Wren frowned and shook her head. Right now she wouldn't think about Paula. The people in the Wheeler house were more important.

Smells of fried chicken and freshly cooked string beans drifted out to her as she walked through the utility room into the kitchen. Maybe her family wouldn't be too upset that she was late again.

"Hi, everyone. Sorry I'm late." Her strong, white teeth glistened in her suntanned face as she flashed the brightest smile she could manage. "The chicken smells good, Dad." Dad always fried the chicken with his own special coating. "The salad's beautiful, Mom." Mom always tossed the salad. "Everything looks good." Her smile faded a little as her brothers turned from setting the table. She knew it was her turn.

"All right, Wren, what're you up to this time?" Mom stood beside the table with her hands on her slender hips, her head tilted. She still wore the same blue dress that Wren knew she'd worn in court today when she'd argued her cases.

Wren put on her most innocent face. "What do you mean, Mom?"

"I can tell that you're up to something."

Dad laughed and tapped Wren's arm. "I'm the detective in this house and I agree with your mother. You look very guilty. What did you do? Call the school and tell them that Paula Gantz is really a grown woman in a child's body and is too old to attend JCA?"

Wren gasped and clutched her throat. "Do you mean Paula told me the truth? Is she really going to JCA?"

"She is," said Mom with a nod. "And you are going to be kind to her because that's what Jesus wants."

Wren nodded, but her shoulders drooped.

"Hey, look!" cried Philip as he glanced out the window. "Someone's going into Mrs. Wheeler's place."

"That's impossible!" Mom peered out the window with a frown. "Sam, what do you know about this?"

"Not a thing, Lorrene. I think after we eat I'll give Mrs. Wheeler a call and find out."

"I wonder if they have kids," said Philip. Wren knew he meant girls. She almost let it slip that they had a boy and that he might be in danger, but she caught herself in time. Although she knew her mom appreciated her taking care of the house for Mrs. Wheeler, she didn't want her brothers to know that she often went in just to be alone.

"Maybe I should go pay them a visit," said Mom.

"We could ask Paula," said Neil with a grin.

Philip laughed and punched Neil's arm. "She knows everything about everybody before they know it themselves." At sixteen Philip was tall and lean and good looking with dark red hair and hazel eyes. Wren's friends envied her because she saw him all the time. She didn't know why they thought he was so great.

"Mom, may I go with you to see the neighbors?" asked

Wren as she sat in her place at the table.

"If you're home."

Wren touched the key in her pocket and her heart jerked a funny little jerk at the idea that she'd suddenly had. Dare she watch the house and then sneak inside when the man and woman went away? They had to get groceries sometime. Maybe she could slip inside and talk to the boy—even set him free if he really had been kidnapped!

Shivers ran up and down her spine as she bowed her head while Neil asked the blessing on the food.

2

FIRST DAY OF SCHOOL

Wren pushed her red and white book bag back onto her shoulder as she ran across her yard the next morning. Inside the bag she carried her Bible, pencils, notebooks, ball-point pens and a small pack of Kleenex in case she started sneezing the way she sometimes did. She slowed to a walk when she reached Mrs. Wheeler's yard. Would the new people object to her cutting across the lawn? She looked toward the wide front window and the heavy oak door beside it. The Wheeler place was built toward the back of the lot. Flowers bloomed along the edge of the sidewalk that led to the garage. A robin flew from one bush to another. A boy on a bicycle whizzed past on the street.

Just then the front door opened and the man and woman Wren had seen yesterday walked out. They stopped when they saw Wren and she managed to smile. The woman wore a white nurse's uniform and the man was dressed in the same jeans and black polo shirt. They stared at Wren, then finally the man smiled.

"Good morning. It's a beautiful morning, isn't it?"

Wren's stomach knotted nervously, but she managed to nod and smile. "I'm Wren House and I live next door. I'm on my way to school. I didn't know Mrs. Wheeler had anyone living in her house." Wren saw the quick look that darted between the man and woman.

The woman stepped toward Wren with a smile that didn't reach her blue eyes. "You must be the little Wren that Grandma talks about! I'm Illa Wheeler and this is my husband Jeff. Mrs. Wheeler is our grandma and she gave us permission to stay in her house until she's well enough to come home."

Wren wanted to believe them, but somehow she couldn't. "I thought you lived in Illinois."

"We do. We did," answered the man. "But when Grandma had her stroke, we couldn't leave her here all alone." His eyes narrowed. "Do you take care of the place for her?" Wren nodded.

"Then you must have a key. Give it to us and we'll take care of the house." The man waited and tension crackled in the air.

"Mom has the key," said Wren breathlessly. Her key was safely tucked away in her secret box in her dresser drawer. "And she already left for the courthouse."

"The courthouse?" The woman moved her purse from one hand to another.

"She's a lawyer. And my dad's a private detective. He has ways of finding out everything about everybody." Wren watched for a reaction and she thought she saw fear in the man's eyes, but she couldn't be sure.

"That's very interesting," said the woman. "I'm a nurse in Illinois and Jeff works on construction when he can. "

"Do you have any kids?" Wren kept her voice light although she felt goosebumps on her arms as she waited for an answer.

"No. We don't have any kids," said the woman sharply. "Now, I think you'd better get on your way to school."

Wren dashed off, her head spinning. They were lying! They really were. She had seen them drag a boy through the house, his stick arms almost popping from their sockets as they pulled on him. Why, oh why, did she have to go to school right when the man and woman were leaving? How she wanted to run back home, grab her key and investigate the Wheeler place. Would she find the boy tied to his bed? Or maybe asleep from a sleeping pill they'd forced him to take?

"There you are, Wren! I wondered what was taking you so long." Bess called out to Wren as she came out of her house. She carried her blue book bag and Wren knew it held almost the same things as hers did. Bess's blonde hair was feathered back from her face. "Aren't you going to speak to me, Wren?" Bess shook Wren's arm.

Wren nudged Bess. "Don't look now, but someone's

living in the Wheeler place and something funny is going on." Bess looked toward the Wheeler garage. "What's so funny? That man and woman look ordinary to me."

Wren pulled Bess around her house to the sidewalk. Wren smiled. "I've found a mystery and I'm going to solve it."

"Oh, Wren, you're always finding a mystery. So far, all of your mysteries have turned out to be nothing."

Wren frowned and pushed the strap of her book bag farther onto her shoulder. What Bess had said was true, but this time she knew that this was a real mystery.

"We have to hurry, Wren. We can't be late our first day."

Nodding agreement, Wren pushed the mystery to the back of her mind and ran to school with Bess. Just outside the long brick building she stopped Bess. "Did you hear about Paula Gantz?"

"What about her?" Bess glanced at Wren, then looked around for Neil.

"She's coming to school here."

The color drained from Bess's face. "What? Are you sure?"

"I'm sure. Mom says I have to be nice to her."

"Well, I'm not going to be! She thinks Neil likes her. She's so dumb! Neil wouldn't go out with her. Would he?"

"Never!"

Bess sighed and pressed her hand over her heart. "I

didn't think so."

"There's the bell. Come on." Wren dashed into the school and down the hall to the fifth grade room. Boys and girls laughed and talked. Someone bumped against Wren just as she stepped into the fifth grade room. She glanced back to find Tim Avery grinning at her. Anger rushed through her and she pressed her lips shut tightly to keep back sharp words. He looked almost the same as last year and she wondered if he'd changed his jeans and shirt or taken a shower all summer. His red hair did look clean and newly cut. He was a little taller, too, almost as tall as Bess.

Wren dropped down in a seat behind Bess, ignoring Tim. He sat in a desk to her right. She looked away from him only to find Paula in the desk to her left. Her heart sank to her feet and her stomach knotted into an icy ball.

Another bell rang and everyone grew quiet. A tall, slender woman walked to the front of the room. She wore a burgundy skirt and vest with a white blouse. Her light brown hair curled around her attractive face and hung to her shoulders. Wren caught a faint whiff of her perfume and liked it.

"Good morning, class. I know that you were all expecting Mrs. Lincoln, but she and her husband moved a couple of weeks ago and I was called in. My name is Meg Brewster and you can call me Miss Brewster." She turned with a flourish and wrote it on the board. Wren's heart sank. She had been so sure that Mrs. Lincoln would be here. Miss Brewster turned back and picked up a record book. "I'll call off your names and as I say your name, raise your hand and say 'here'."

Wren locked her hands in her lap and waited as Miss Brewster went down the list. She hesitated when she reached the Hs.

"There seems to be a typo here, " she said with a frown. "Wren House, it says."

Wren raised her hand. It was always the same with someone new. "Here," she said in a tiny voice.

"Wren House?"

The usual snicker went around the room and Wren noticed that Paula laughed outright.

"My mother named me," said Wren, lifting her chin a fraction.

Miss Brewster's face turned pink and she cleared her throat. "Yes, well, that is a very unusual name. But it is eye-catching, and often that's important in the occupation you choose." She cleared her throat and went to the next name. Wren sank back with a sigh.

"Wren House," whispered Paula. "Bird House."

Wren glared at her and she whispered it again. Wren struggled against the anger that almost overwhelmed her. Right now she needed help from the Lord so that she wouldn't leap on Paula and stuff her book bag in her mouth. Wren knew that God was always there to help her and right now she desperately needed help. Silently she prayed, and she felt the anger begin to wash away as the Lord answered.

Later, during English class, Miss Brewster glanced around the class with a happy look on her face. "I have an assignment to give you that I think you'll find very enjoyable." The class whispered, then grew quiet. "It'll take team work away from school and you'll have two weeks to complete it. "

Bess turned and smiled at Wren and they both nodded. They always worked on things together.

"Each team will make a movie showing a Biblical principle in action." Miss Brewster turned to the board and wrote as she talked. "Here are a few ideas, or you can find one of your own and film it. Be kind. Love your neighbors. Give. Feed and clothe the poor and needy. Tell others about Jesus. The school's video department will furnish a camcorder to each team that needs one."

Wren smiled, barely able to sit still. She was good at making movies, and it would be fun to do one as an assignment. Maybe they'd take be kind, or even love your neighbor. She thought about the people in the Wheeler house. It was hard to think of them as the Wheelers. This would be a good way to watch the Wheelers and solve the mystery as well as make the movie.

"We need three in each group," Miss Brewster said.

Tim waved his arm frantically.

"Yes, Tim."

"I want to be with Wren and Bess."

Wren's heart sank and she frowned at Tim. He smiled at her and his blue eyes sparkled.

"Wren, Bess, and Tim. Yes, that's fine. Anyone else have a preference? If not, I'll assign you." Several hands shot up and Miss Brewster was kept busy writing down the teams.

Wren leaned toward Tim and whispered, "Why did you do that? You could be on a team with Russ and Sean."

"I wanted to work with you. I'd be good with a camcorder and I know you are."

Bess turned around. "I guess we have to let him work with us," she whispered.

"We don't have a choice," said Wren. Maybe there wouldn't be a problem. Tim lived across town, too far away to work with them. He probably hadn't thought about that. She looked at Tim and smiled smugly. He grinned back, happy as a kid in a room full of computers. "You'll never be able to come to my house since you live so far away, Tim."

Tim shrugged. "Mr. Landon bought me a ten speed bike and I can go anywhere now." Suddenly Wren hated Mr. Adam Landon and wished he'd lose all of his money, or forget all about Tim Avery. Why did he have to pay Tim's way to JCA?

Just then the bell rang for recess. Wren grabbed Bess

and rushed out of the room, down the hall and out into the bright sunlight. She sneezed, then sneezed again.

"I think I'll go to public school," she muttered as she pulled a tissue from her pocket. But she knew she wouldn't. She'd attended JCA since kindergarten and she'd stay until she graduated from high school. But with Tim and Paula around year after year, it wouldn't be easy.

"Let's go swing and talk," said Bess.

Wren followed her across the playground with her head down and her shoulders drooping.

3

A FACE IN THE WINDOW

Wren held the camcorder to her eye and started recording as she walked across her backyard toward Bess who waved and danced around. They were using a tape from the House's last weekend vacation that hadn't been completely used.

Wren turned the camera away from Bess to the Wheeler house—and her breath caught in her throat. There was a face in the window. It was the little boy, pale and frightened. Then, he was gone. Wren wondered if she's really seen him. She lowered the camera and tried to speak, but no words came out.

"Did you see him, Wren?" Bess gripped Wren's arm and shook it. "Did you see a boy in that window?"

Wren nodded, her face pale. "I did and then I think someone jerked him away." When Wren had told Bess about the man, woman and the boy, Bess had stopped teasing her about finding another mystery. She had offered to help solve it. "I bet they did kidnap him."

Bess rubbed her hand across her damp forehead. "I'm

scared. Let's talk to your dad."

"We can't right now. A client is with him." Wren's dad had an office in the house with an outside door of its own. "Besides, it would be fun to solve this on our own without Dad's help."

"But he's a detective and he knows how to handle these things." Bess swallowed hard as she looked toward the Wheeler place.

Wren frowned as she leaned against the picnic table, the camera beside her. "We could ask his advice without telling him that we're the ones solving the mystery."

She knew she'd have to be very careful since she'd already talked to him about the people in the Wheeler house. He had called Mrs. Wheeler and learned that she had, indeed, invited her grandson and his wife to stay at her house. She said she'd sent them a key. To Dad the case was solved and the man and woman were Jeff and Illa Wheeler. But Wren knew that they had called each other George and Jan. And they had lied about the boy in the bedroom.

"Let's wait by the door so when his client comes out, we can go right in." Bess tugged on Wren's arm, but she twisted free.

"We can work on our project while we're waiting."

"Tim's not here."

"Who cares?" Wren picked up the camera again and pointed it toward the Wheeler place just as the man walked out. He saw her with the camera and jumped back inside, slamming the door. "Did you see that, Bess?"

hissed Wren, tingling with excitement. "He's guilty all right. Why else would he hide from the camera?"

"Let's get out of here!" Bess ran toward the back door of Wren's home. "Come on, Wren!" Wren hesitated, then ran after Bess. The tape was finished anyway. They had to put in a new tape in order to do their school project.

Inside, the house was cool and quiet. Both boys were with friends and wouldn't be home until almost dinner time. They'd both reminded Wren that it was her turn to help with dinner and to set the table.

Bess peeked out the window and watched as the neighbor man walked to his car and drove away. "He's gone, Wren. We can go back outdoors now."

Wren pressed close to the window. "I wonder if they're both gone. This would be a good time to get inside and check on her boy."

Even as she spoke her skin tingled with excitement and fear. Would she dare walk into the Wheeler house now and look around? "Shall we go look, Bess?"

"Oh, my! I don't know. What if they catch us inside? What if they grab us and hold us prisoner?"

"I could go inside and you could be the look-out.

"Bess gasped and fell back a step, bumping into the kitchen table. "I could never do that!"

Wren ran to the den for the new cassette tape and quickly loaded the camcorder. She stuck the finished tape on the shelf behind a ceramic blue bird that she'd done in class last year. Running around the coffee table, she called for Bess to follow her. Mom's copy of Mrs. Wheeler's key hung with the other keys near the back door. Wren pushed it into the pocket of her tan slacks as she ran outdoors with the camcorder. Bess ran out behind her.

"I mean it, Wren. I won't stand outside that door while you sneak inside. You can't make me."

"Then come inside with me."

"Me!" Bess's eyes widened and she shook her head. "No, no! And I don't think you should go inside. Let your dad do it."

Wren stopped with an impatient frown. "Can't you ever do anything daring? You're too careful."

"But I stay out of trouble. My parents aren't always yelling at me for getting into embarrassing situations."

"Meaning mine do?"

"Yes." Wren turned away and Bess caught at her arm. "You know it's true. Everyone knows it is. Don't get mad at me for speaking the truth."

"We're wasting time, Bess. If you don't want to come with me or be a guard for me, then sit down in the back yard and stay out of the way." Wren ran into the Wheeler's yard and stopped at the side door. She listened at the door, her heart racing. Before she could slip the key into the lock, a car pulled in and stopped outside the garage. Wren's heart sank and she looked around wildly for a place to hide. But it was too late. Jeff and Illa Wheeler were getting out of the car and looking right at her. Instantly she lifted the camcorder up and pushed the record button.

"Hey, don't do that, kid!" The man ducked his head to hide from the camera.

"Just what do you think you're doing?" snapped the woman. She looked tired and her uniform was soiled. "Give me that camera. You have no business taking our picture!"

Wren backed away and almost tripped. She held the camcorder to her, shielding it from the woman. "We're working on a school project. We're taking pictures of our neighbors to show how we can help them." She looked around for Bess, but she was cowering by Wren's back door. Her face was red with embarrassment. She was no help at all.

"Give me that camera!" The man reached for Wren, but she jumped out of his way. "We'll take the tape and give you money to cover it. We don't like our pictures taken." He glared at Wren. "Hey, didn't I see you with that camera before I left to pick up my wife from the hospital?"

Wren shrugged. She wanted to dash around them and get to the safety of her yard, but she didn't want them to become suspicious of her. "It's a school assignment. But I won't take pictures of you if you don't want. I'll find another neighbor."

"I want that cassette!" The woman grabbed for the camera just as Tim Avery rode up beside Wren. The woman jumped back to keep Tim from running into her with his bike.

"Hi, Wren." Tim grinned at her and for once she was glad to see him. "Started our school project already, I see. Let me have the camera and I'll ride across the street and film the family there. I just saw them drive in." He plucked the camera from her and rode away, leaving the Wheelers fuming.

"I'll help you, Tim." Wren started past the woman, but she grabbed Wren's arm and jerked her up short. Wren yelped in surprise and pain.

"I talked to your mother this morning and she said she'd give us the house key. I want it now before you get any ideas about sneaking into our house." Illa Wheeler held out her hand and glared at Wren as if daring Wren to defy her.

Slowly Wren reaching into her pocket and held out the key. "I'll tell Mom that I brought it to you. She left it beside the back door."

"Yes, you do that." The woman grabbed the key and dropped it into her pocket, then turned to her husband. "Let's get inside. If you ever see this kid sneaking around taking pictures of us again, stop her. Tell her parents or something."

Mr. Wheeler nodded. He followed his wife toward the front door, then turned back to Wren. "We hate having our pictures taken. You can understand that, can't you? We want to wait until we're cleaned up and looking our best before anyone takes pictures of us."

Wren nodded as she locked her trembling hands behind her back. When the door closed she ran to her yard to find Tim there with Bess. Without a word Tim held the camera out to Wren.

"I filmed them yelling at you," he said quietly, more serious than she'd ever seen him. "In case you ever have to prove that they were mean to you."

She shook her head, surprised that Tim would think of that. "I can't believe they were that upset. They act like they have something to hide."

"Like that boy hidden inside," said Bess.

Wren shot her a look and Bess ducked her head.

"Is there a boy hidden inside that house?" Tim looked toward the blue frame house with interest. "Is there a mystery right next door?"

Wren stared at him in surprise, trying to tell if he was making fun of her. But he seemed serious and she cleared her throat. "Bess talks too much."

"Is there a boy hidden inside that house?" Tim stepped close to Wren and looked intently at her. "Is there?"

Finally, she nodded. Then, before she could stop herself, she told him what she'd seen and heard. "They said they were the Wheelers and that they didn't have any children."

Tim stroked his chin thoughtfully. "Very interesting. I'm glad this school assignment will keep me around here a lot so that I can help solve this case."

Bess groaned. "I still say we should tell your dad, Wren."

"No!" cried Tim, looking from Bess to Wren. "This is something we can handle by ourselves."

Wren tilted her head and finally grinned at Tim. "Yes. Yes, it is. But right now, let's get started on our project about helping our neighbors."

4

A VISIT WITH MRS. WHEELER

Wren glanced at the Wheeler house. Solving a mystery was more important than doing her school project. Tim leaned against the picnic table with his arms crossed over his thin chest and looked at Wren and Bess. "I think we should go have a long talk with Mrs. Wheeler at the hospital. We can work on our project another day."

"We could ride our bikes there." Wren's dark eyes sparkled and she walked back and forth on the grass. "Let's go right now before dinnertime."

Bess shook her head. "You're both crazy! They won't let you into her room. They won't let you talk to her."

"I'll get in to talk to her, and I'll learn the truth. Maybe she misunderstood Dad when he talked to her on the phone last night."

Bess stood with her fists on her thin hips, and her feet apart. "I thought we were going to work together on a school project. I don't want to fail the class, you know. It's important to me to get a good grade in everything that I do."

"We'll get the tape done, Bess. You don't have to worry. It's just that some things are more important." Tim smiled at Wren. "Like solving a mystery."

"Exactly," said Wren, changing her mind about Tim even more. He was still dirty and it still embarrassed her to have him hanging around her, but he was smart about some things. "I'll put the camera inside and get my bike. Be right back, Tim."

He nodded.

"I'm going home," snapped Bess. She pushed back her blonde hair and walked away in a huff. Wren watched her go, then ran to the house to put the camera on the utility room table.

Soon she was riding toward the hospital with Tim a few feet in front of her. The wind blew his red hair and puffed out his tee shirt. Suddenly Wren didn't care if her friends from school saw them together. They were on a secret mission and that was more important than what anyone thought. Wren laughed.

At the hospital they parked at the bike stands and looked toward the heavy glass doors. An ambulance drove up the drive and stopped outside the emergency entrance. They saw people walking to their cars and others walking toward the doors to visit someone inside.

"Let's go," said Tim, sounding confident and sure.

Her stomach fluttered, but she squared her shoulders. "Let's go," she replied. But she couldn't move. "I'll ask her all about her grandson and his wife. Dad says she can't talk very fast after her stroke, and that she gets upset with herself. I'll have to be careful with her."

"You'll do just fine." Tim smiled. "You will. I know it."

She flushed with pleasure, squared her shoulders again and walked right up to the heavy glass door and inside. The cool air felt great after the hot ride. The smells sickened her for a minute, but she kept walking as if she knew right where she was going. Tim walked along beside her, his tennis shoes as quiet on the floor as hers.

At the elevators she pushed the button for the fourth floor, and they rode up in silence. Stepping out when the doors opened, they stood beside the wall, looking toward the nurse's station. Mrs. Wheeler's room was 402. It was just on the other side of the station. Dad had told her where it was when Mrs. Wheeler was admitted.

"I'll keep them talking while you go in," whispered Tim as he hiked up his jeans.

"I won't stay long." Butterflies fluttered in her stomach. Someone down the hall laughed. Wren waited until Tim stopped at the station and asked the nurse something. The nurse behind the desk turned to look at the monitor that Tim was pointing at. Wren slipped past the desk and into the room where Mrs. Wheeler lay.

The old woman looked pale and different. Wren barely recognized her. The smell of the room sickened Wren. She wanted to turn and run, but she forced herself to walk right up to the side of the narrow bed. "Hello, Mrs. Wheeler," she said softly.

Mrs. Wheeler opened her eyes and smiled, then opened her mouth to speak. A few seconds later she managed to say, "Wren?" Tears filled Mrs. Wheeler's faded gray eyes. "I miss you."

"I miss you, too." Wren lifted the frail hand and looked down at it. Blue veins stood out on the white soft hand. "I came to talk to you about your grandson, Jeff."

"Yes, Jeff." Mrs. Wheeler's voice was low and unsteady.

"Do you have a picture of him?"

"Purse. In my purse. There." Her hand trembled as she pointed to the bedside stand.

"Does he have children?"

"No."

Wren pulled out the purse and looked inside. She found the folder of photos and handed them to Mrs. Wheeler. "Did he and his wife come to visit you yet?"

"Yes, but I was asleep."

"Asleep? Then how do you know they came?"

Mrs. Wheeler dropped the folder and Wren picked it up. "Nurse Bliss told me. They left the flowers."

Wren touched the petal of a bright yellow mum and read the card. It was from Jeff and Illa. "I'll flip through the pictures and you tell me when I come to Jeff."

"I'm not as strong as I once was."

"But you will be." It frightened Wren to see her friend

looking so old and worn out. It was hard to understand every word she said. "Hey, some pictures are missing. Maybe they fell out inside your purse." Wren looked, but no photos were there. "None of these are Jeff and Illa?"

"None."

"Did you send them your house key?"

"Yes. Nurse Bliss sent it with a letter she wrote for me." Mrs. Wheeler moved restlessly. "I hope I'm awake when they come to see me tonight."

"You should ask the nurse to wake you up."

Mrs. Wheeler smiled shakily. "I will."

"I saw Jeff and Illa at your house. They had a boy with them." Wren waited, barely breathing.

"I remember." She moved her mouth and finally the words followed. "They are taking care of Illa's nephew for a while. I told them I didn't mind if they had a child in my house. I like children."

Wren sighed in relief then in disappointment. She leaned over and kissed the paper thin cheek. "I'd better go now. You come home soon and I'll fix you a pot of your favorite tea."

"Thank you." Mrs. Wheeler's eyes fluttered closed and Wren tiptoed out and peeked down the hall. Tim saw her and turned back to talk to the nurse again. Wren slipped past them and waited for Tim at the elevators.

"Well?" Tim's cheeks were flushed with excitement and he could barely stand still while the elevator doors slid open.

Wren stepped inside and waited until the doors closed. "Well nothing! Mrs. Wheeler didn't have pictures of Jeff and Illa. She said the boy is Illa's nephew. Mrs. Wheeler said they came to visit her, but she was asleep."

"The end of a mystery." Tim sagged back against the elevator's shiny bar and sighed."The end of a mystery," whispered Wren. Tears stung her eyes and she turned away before Tim saw them.

They rode in silence to the main floor, then walked down the hall to the doors. Heat hit them as they walked to their bikes. Wren glanced at her watch and her heart sank. She was going to be too late to help with dinner again.

"See you in school tomorrow, Wren."

"See you, Tim—and thanks." He stood beside his bike with a thoughtful look on his face. A siren wailed in the distance, going away from the hospital.

"We could get inside her house and look for pictures of Jeff and Illa. She'd probably have some."

"We could, but why bother?"

He shrugged.

"I'd better get home."

"Yeah, me, too. I'm sorry, Wren."

"For what?" But she knew.

"For the end of a good mystery."

"The end for sure." She sighed, then rode toward home.

5

VIDEO TAPE

Wren sat on the picnic table with her feet on the bench and the camcorder on her lap. "You don't have to worry, Bess. I found out yesterday that it really is Jeff and Illa staying there." Wren nodded toward the Wheeler place. "Tim and I know there isn't a mystery now, so we can all three work together on our movie and you can get your good grade."

Bess watched the back door of Wren's house. "Is Neil home yet?"

"He's at Brian's house." Wren had wanted to beg Neil to bring Brian home, but she'd forced back the words. No way did she want Neil or anyone else except Bess to know that she liked Brian Davies.

"I wish they were both here. We could tape them and tell them it's a school project." Bess fluffed her hair and looked dreamy. "I get so tired of waiting to grow up. I want to go out with Neil. I want to get kissed. Doesn't it sound romantic? I've been watching people kiss on TV so that when I'm allowed to, I'll know how."

"I don't think kissing is such a big deal." Wren was glad that she couldn't go with boys until she was fifteen and couldn't kiss one until she was sixteen. It was a lot more fun to solve a mystery than to be kissed. She glanced at her watch. "What's keeping Tim? He said he'd be here before four and it's already five after."

Just then the Wheelers drove in and walked into the house without a wave or a hello. As Wren sighed and turned away, Tim whirled around the house. He leaped off his bike and leaned it against the end of the picnic table. His face was as red as his hair and his blue tee shirt was damp with perspiration.

"You're late," said Bess.

He ignored her and smiled at Wren. "I followed them." He nodded toward the Wheeler place. "She works at the hospital. Would Illa Wheeler already have a job at the hospital if she just moved here from Illinois?"

Wren clutched the camcorder tighter as excitement bubbled inside her.

"They were at the hospital to visit Mrs. Wheeler," said Bess impatiently. "You don't have to be smart to figure that out."

Wren shook her head. "She's probably right."

"Then why did she have on a uniform? A nurse's uniform?"

"She's a nurse in Illinois. Maybe she got transferred

here." Wren shrugged. "I don't know! Or maybe she wears it so she can help out with her grandma while she's there."

Tim's face fell and he jabbed his fingers through his red hair. "You could be right. But I think it would be smart to have a picture to show at the hospital and that way we'd know for sure. We can use your camera and take a snapshot of her." Wren thoughtfully studied the Wheeler place. Had she given up too soon? It would be fun to take a photo of Illa Wheeler to the hospital and show it around. Dad did that kind of thing often. Suddenly the day was bright and beautiful. Wren threw back her head and laughed. Bess frowned, but Tim's laughter joined hers.

"I have some families lined up," said Bess. "We have to get to work! We'll film them helping their neighbors to get across our main theme of loving your neighbor as yourself."

At the Duncans' house, Wren filmed the five Duncan children along with Mr. and Mrs. Duncan helping the neighbors paint their house. At Birta's, Bess and Wren helped pick tomatoes from the garden while Tim ran the camera. Down the street they filmed Betty Dandron taking a chocolate cake to her neighbor who was having company for dinner. Bess filmed Ann Arnett inviting the neighborhood children to her house to swim with her children. Wren finished up the tape showing two old men talking together over a game of chess. She figured loving meant also giving time and friendship.

"We did a great job," said Wren with pride as they walked toward her house. "That should easily give us all an A."

"It should," said Bess with a pleased smile.

"Bess, it was really smart of you to line it all up so that we could just go in and shoot the scenes," added Tim.

Bess flushed with pleasure. "Thanks."

"We're a good team," said Wren. To her surprise she found that she meant it. She'd enjoyed working with Bess and Tim. Too bad she hadn't taken time to get to know Tim last year. She'd wasted a whole year hating him when all the time they could've been friends.

Just then Paula Gantz called to them and waved. She held a video camera and looked very pleased with herself. "I already have my tape finished. Joyce and Tina worked with me. I bet we get the best grade and have the best movie in the whole class."

Wren rolled her eyes and shook her head. "We have ours finished, too. It'll be good."

"The best," said Bess smugly.

"They can't all be the best. In public school I was always at the head of my class and I know I will be at JCA, too." Paula narrowed her dark eyes. "I'm always the best!"

"Oh, sure," said Tim with a chuckle. "See you in school tomorrow. Right now we have to get the tape to Mr. House. He'll edit it for us."

Paula tossed her head back. "Oh, sure, get somebody to help you. Did he help take the video, too?"

Wren nudged Bess and Tim. "Let's go. We don't want to fight with anyone." She saw the anger flare from Paula's eyes before she walked away with Bess and Tim.

At the back door Tim asked, "Did your dad edit the other tape yet?"

"He said he would. We could ask him now. I don't think he has a client."

They ran around to Sam House's office door and knocked, then opened the door when he called, "Come in."

"Hi, Dad. Bess and Tim and I finished the tape. Did you get the other one edited?"

Sam walked toward the group with a slow smile. He was tall and lean with brown hair and eyes. "I thought I'd wait and do the two at the same time." He held out his hand for the camera and Wren handed it to him. He opened it to take out the tape, then frowned. "What's the joke, kids?"

"What?" asked Wren as Tim and Bess stepped closer.

"There's no cassette in here." Sam turned so they could see.

"That's impossible!" Wren shook her head as Tim and Bess both talked at once. "It was in there yesterday when we filmed . . . " Their voices died away and Wren jabbed Tim with her elbow."

"Do you think. . . ?" Tim's eyes sparkled and Wren

knew that he was thinking that the mystery was on.

"I bet Paula took it out," said Bess. "I bet she did so that we couldn't make our video."

Wren closed her eyes and moaned. She'd much rather think the neighbors had taken it than Paula. There'd be no excitement in it if Paula had taken it out of jealousy or anger.

"Now we'll have to shoot the whole thing over again!" cried Bess. "I can't believe this is happening!"

Sam leaned back against his desk and crossed his ankles. "I've known Paula all her life and I don't believe she'd sneak into the house and take the tape out of the camera. It's not her style. But she might know who did."

Wren giggled. "She might." She turned to Tim. "Paula knows everything that goes on around here."

"That's the truth," said Bess, nodding. "But I'd hate to ask her about this and have her find out that we taped all those people without a cassette."

Sam laughed. "You've got a point there." He waved toward the leather couch. "Have a seat and let's do some deductive reasoning."

Wren liked the sound of that, and she perched on the edge of the blue leather couch with Bess and Tim beside her. "We should first decide who had access to the camera."

"And then decide which of that list wouldn't bother it," added Tim.

Wren looked at him in awe. He sure knew about deductive reasoning.

Wren's dad made out a list of the people in a battered notebook that he'd picked up off his desk. "We know that no one in the House family would touch the tape."

Wren nodded. "Nor would Neil's or Philip's friends in case they came when we didn't know they were here."

"I could've done it," said Bess, "but I didn't. And Tim didn't. Who else could've gone into the house to take it?"

"Where did you leave the camera, Wren?" asked Mr. House.

Wren gripped her bare knees. "I left it in the utility room and anyone looking in the back door could see it. But if anyone peeked in with robbery in mind, they'd take the camera, not the cassette."

"That's right," said Tim. "The one who took it was only interested in the tape and the only thing on it was the new neighbors."

"Very interesting," said Wren's dad, rubbing a suntanned hand over his dark hair. "But why would they object to being on tape?"

Wren knew a good reason, but she didn't want to get her dad suspicious or he'd start investigating and she wouldn't have a chance. She shot a look at Tim and Bess to keep them from talking. It worked. Everyone was silent. The clock tick-tocked on the shelf beside the door and a car honked outdoors.

Sam walked across the room. "I'll get that other tape edited for you and get you a new cassette. I'm sorry, but it looks like you'll have to film a whole new movie for your project."

Bess groaned. "I don't have time to do any more today. We'll have to work on it tomorrow, I guess. I hope all those people will let us film them again." She told them all goodbye and walked out

"Wren, take Tim to the kitchen for a cookie," said Mr. House. "I'm sorry all your work was for nothing today."

"Yeah, me too," said Wren. She led Tim to the kitchen and they sat at the table with milk and chocolate chip cookies that Neil had baked. "I bet that man took the cassette. Or the woman."

"The Wheelers?"

"They aren't really the Wheelers." Wren laughed softly and Tim grinned.

"The investigation is on, Wren."

6

PLANS

Wren jumped up and twirled around, then dropped back on the kitchen chair. "We've got to make some plans."

Tim leaned back in the kitchen chair with his hands locked behind his head and his skinny arms jabbing the air. "We have to find a way into that house while the Wheelers, or whoever they are, are gone."

Wren twisted her glass of milk. "I have a key." Her voice was low and strained.

Tim jerked forward. "A key?"

Wren nodded. "To the side door. Mrs. Wheeler gave Mom a key and I had it copied so that I could get inside when I wanted if Mom had her key in her purse."

"That's great!" Tim laughed and slapped the table. "That is really great! We'll watch the house and go inside while they're gone."

"The only time that they're gone is when we're in school or I'd have already gone inside to see about that boy."

"Then we'll have to find a way to get them out." Tim

narrowed his eyes and drummed his fingers on the table.

Wren swallowed the rest of her milk and wiped the back of her hand across her mouth. "I wonder if they plan to go visit Mrs. Wheeler in the hospital tonight. We need to find out." Her face lit up. "I have it! Let's pick a bouquet of flowers and take them to Jeff and Illa. Then we can ask if they'd take them to their grandma when they visit her tonight. If they aren't going, they'll tell us."

"Let's go."

Wren ran out into the yard and picked gold and yellow marigolds as well as orange and red and yellow zinnias. She held them away from her nose and admired their beauty as she tried not to breathe in their strong aroma. "We'll get them to talk about their home in Illinois."

"Good idea. Do you know where they live? We could call there and see if anyone answers."

Wren frowned thoughtfully as she watched a bug crawl down a flower stem. "Mrs. Wheeler told me, but I can't remember. I could call her and ask."

"We should've thought of that right away."

"You're right. I guess this all takes practice." Wren smiled as Tim grinned and nodded. "Let's go." Wren's stomach cramped and for one wild minute she was afraid, and then she squared her shoulders and strode across the yard with Tim beside her. She rang the doorbell and waited, the flowers clutched in her small, brown hand.

Tim leaned his head against the door. "Someone's

coming." He jumped back to stand beside Wren, a very innocent look on his freckled face.

The door burst open and the woman stood there dressed in jeans and a Mickey Mouse tee shirt. Her eyes looked cold and Wren almost turned away.

"I brought these for your grandma." Wren thrust them forward and the woman took them. "Will you give them to her when you visit her tonight?"

"Jeff might go alone." Illa started to close the door.

"Wait!" Wren cleared her throat. "Never mind. My dad's planning on visiting her after dinner. He'll take them."

The woman moistened her lips with the tip of her tongue. "Tell your dad that Grandma's not up to seeing visitors outside the family. I'll take the flowers to her tomorrow.

"Me and Wren will take them to the hospital right now and deliver them." Tim reached for the flowers, but Illa jerked them out of his reach.

"I'll take them to her tonight."

"Do you live near Chicago?" asked Wren.

Illa frowned. "Evanston."

"I forgot."

"I've been to the museum in Chicago once," said Tim. "It was great."

"We're right in the middle of dinner." Illa started to close the door.

"Tell Mrs. Wheeler we'll call her after awhile to see how she likes them," said Wren.

"There is absolutely no need for you to call Grandma! She needs her rest. In fact, I've asked the doctor to take her phone away."

Wren looked at Tim for an answer and he spoke right up.

"Tell Mrs. Wheeler that the flowers are from Wren and I'm sure she'll want to call or send a message through you. We won't be satisfied until we know that she's gotten the flowers."

"That's right. We won't," said Wren firmly.

The woman nodded and a muscle jumped in her neck.

"We'll wait right in my yard so that we know when you leave." Wren smiled and backed away. "That way I'll know not to get too impatient and call her anyway."

Illa slammed the door shut. Wren and Tim ran back to Wren's yard. Wren forced back a wild whoop and Tim fell to the ground laughing. He jumped up with a twig stuck in his hair.

"Go get your key while I keep watch," he said. He jumped up on the picnic table and faced the Wheeler place. "Surveillance right out in the open. What would your dad think of that?"

"He might decide to hire us to work for him." She said it as a joke, but it had always been one of her greatest desires and dreams.

"I'd like that." Tim nodded. "I would really like that. I bet I could do a good job, too. And I know you would since you've lived with your dad and watched him work and listened to his great stories."

Wren heard the envy in Tim's voice and she wondered if he wished he had a detective for a dad or if he just wished he had a dad.

She ran to the house for the key. How would it feel not to have a dad? How would it feel not to have a mom who made sure you were clean and neat when you left the house? The thoughts were so new and strange to her that she couldn't imagine how it would be.

She found the key and stuck it in the pocket of her jeans, then ran out to rejoin Tim. "Does your mother expect you home for dinner soon?"

He shrugged. "I fix my own supper, so it won't matter what time I get back."

"Do you know how to cook?" Wren could fry eggs and bacon and make toast, but that was about all.

"I've cooked for myself for a long time. Usually I just make a sandwich or eat a bowl of cereal."

"For dinner?" Wren couldn't imagine that. Her mom and dad insisted on a balanced meal for dinner. Wren glanced at her watch and realized that Mom would be driving in soon. Maybe she could invite Tim to eat with them. Before she could speak, the Wheelers walked out of the house, lifted their hands in a wave and slid into their car.

"There they go," whispered Tim. He tugged at his neckline. "Shall we go?"

"I have the key in my pocket." Wren patted her pocket. Shivers ran up and down her spine and she wondered if Tim was as nervous as she. "I guess we'd better go now."

"I guess we'd better."

Wren looked at Tim and he looked at her. Almost at the same time they both said, "Let's go."

A few minutes later they slipped inside the side door. Wren smelled coffee and pizza. The closed-in smell was gone. The unlived-in feeling was gone, too. "I'll look around and you stand guard," Wren offered.

"We'd better stay together."

She nodded. "You're right. We'll stay together." Her voice cracked and she flushed. Carefully, quietly, she tiptoed down the hall to the bedrooms. One door was open and the room looked worse than Neil's. Mrs. Wheeler would be very angry if she knew her bedroom was a mess. The next door was closed and Wren opened it slowly. It was the bedroom that Mrs. Wheeler used for her handcraft items. Things were scattered everywhere and Wren bit back a strangled cry. Mrs. Wheeler loved her crewl, cross-stitch and needlepoint. How could those people mess everything up like this? It could never be set right without hours of work.

"They're looking for something," whispered Tim. "You don't tear through something like that unless you are."

Wren nodded. She should've thought of that.

Tim opened the last door and they looked inside. Wren expected to see a boy tied to the bed, but the room was empty. It had been slept in and it had been searched, but it was empty. This was the room that Mrs. Wheeler used for guests, but it hadn't been used for as long as Wren could remember. Mrs. Wheeler kept it tidy, she said, in case her son or grandson surprised her. They never did.

Wren peeked inside the bathroom and backed out with a shudder. It smelled as if it hadn't been cleaned in a long time and dirty clothes were piled on the floor near the tub.

Tim tugged on Wren's arm. "Quick. Let's look for pictures. She must've shown you pictures of her family."

Wren nodded. "But they were taken when her son was a boy and her grandson a baby." Wren looked around the living room. Dust and newspapers and clothes littered the place. Food lay on the coffee table. Flies buzzed around it. The picture album that always rested on the coffee table was not in sight. Wren dropped to her knees and peeked under the couch. It wasn't there. She turned to watch Tim look in the small bookcase.

A car door slammed and Wren froze. "They can't be back so soon, can they?" she whispered frantically.

"Come on!" Tim and Wren fled to the side door. Just as the front door opened Tim opened the side door and they slipped out. Tim tugged her around the house and led her right to the front door. Her eyes widened and she stepped back as he rang the doorbell.

The man opened it and Tim said, "We saw you come back. Is Mrs. Wheeler all right?"

"Did you give her the flowers?" asked Wren. Her voice sounded shrill to her ears and she wondered if the man noticed.

"Illa forgot something and we had to come back," said Jeff Wheeler impatiently. "She'd forget her head if it wasn't hooked on."

"What're you telling those kids?" Illa poked her head around the door and frowned. "You kids go home." She pulled Jeff's arm and slammed the door.

Wren hesitated, then slowly walked to her yard with Tim beside her. "What're we going to do now? We didn't have enough time to look everywhere. We need more time."

"I wonder what they're looking for. If they found it, would they leave? Did Mrs. Wheeler ever talk to you about her valuables?"

Wren sank to the picnic bench. "She talked to me about a lot of things."

"Did she have expensive rings? Money hidden around the house? A coin collection? Think Wren!"

Before Wren could answer, the back door opened and her mom stepped out. "Wren, you must come inside and help with dinner now."

"Right now, Mom?"

"Right now!" Lorrene smiled at Tim. "You'll have to excuse Wren, Tim. She'll see you in school tomorrow."

"Maybe I could call you later, Tim."

Tim hesitated, then shook his head. "We'll have to wait and talk in the morning. See ya, Wren. Bye, Mrs. House." He jumped on his bike and rode away.

Wren glanced toward Mrs. Wheeler's house in time to see Jeff and Illa getting into their car. Frustration knotted her stomach. If only she could go right now and look around! "Mom, please give me fifteen minutes and then I'll be in. I'll even take the boys' turns for all the rest of the week. Please?"

Lorrene shook her head. "Not even one second, Wren. You have been late too many times lately. Promptness is a virtue."

Wren knew by the set of her mom's face that she wouldn't give in. With a sigh Wren followed Mom into the house to help with dinner. The important investigation would have to wait until another day. A cold band tightened around her heart. Would she be too late if she waited?

7

TRAPPED

Wren sipped her water as the others at the table talked about their day. The key to the Wheeler house seemed as heavy as the biscuits she'd helped make for dinner. How long would Jeff and Illa be gone? Wren moved restlessly. Maybe she could still get inside the Wheeler house again tonight. Her stomach fluttered. Maybe they'd excuse her from the table if she said she didn't want dessert. She thought of the chocolate pudding with the whipped cream on top and hesitated. It was hard to give that up. Maybe she'd ask if she could eat it for a bedtime snack.

"I edited the tape for you today, Wren." Her dad dabbed his mouth with a paper napkin. "All but the very end is our week-end vacation. The part you took is blurry. You'll have to practice holding the camera steady."

"Can I look at it now?" Wren pushed back her chair, but her mother stopped her.

"Finish your steak and salad first, Wren. What's so important about that tape anyway?"

Wren poked a bite of steak into her mouth so that she wouldn't have to answer and by the time she'd swallowed it, Philip was talking about taking a girl to the school carnival next week.

A few minutes later, Wren excused herself and ran to the den where she pushed the tape into the VCR. She pushed fast forward until she neared the end of the film, then sat back and watched Bess jump and dance around. It was blurry and Wren frowned. She scooted close to the TV to catch a glimpse of the face in the Wheeler window, then stopped the picture and studied it. It was impossible to tell if it was a boy or girl, but it was definitely a child. If anyone tried to say that no child had been inside the house, she'd have proof. She frowned. Who would say that? Who really cared? She popped out the cassette and laid it on top of the recorder. She and Bess and Tim could look at it again, maybe tomorrow after school. She'd have to tell them to hold the camcorder steady so that the tape for the school project wouldn't turn out badly.

The key pressed against her leg. She took a deep breath and ran to the front door, slipping out silently. Could anyone hear the loud thud of her heart? She ran around the house and stopped behind a bush to peer at the Wheeler place. The garage door was closed and she knew Mrs. Wheeler's car would be inside where it had been since she went into the hospital.

The car that Jeff and Illa drove was gone. Wren

swallowed hard and took a deep breath. Her legs trembled as she walked to the front door. She pressed the doorbell and waited. She pressed it again, and waited. No one answered and she zipped around the house, unlocked the side door and walked inside before she lost her courage.

Silence surrounded her. She held her breath and forced her heart to stop hammering. She glanced around. Her video tape lay on the floor beside the couch. So, they had stolen it! Slowly she walked across the messy living room to the hall that led to the bedrooms. The boy had stood at the guest bedroom window when she'd taken the film. That's where she'd start looking. She frowned. What did she expect to find now that she hadn't with Tim? Her time was limited. A shiver ran down her back. If Jeff and Illa caught her inside the house, something dreadful would happen. She just knew it.

She stopped outside the bedroom door, her dark eyes wide with sudden fear. Had they killed the boy? Is that why she and Tim hadn't found him? Would they kill her if they knew she was looking through the house? Fear pricked her skin and she looked back down the hall. Should she run out of here and forget the mystery? This was not a game; it was real life. She shivered and pushed the bedroom door open wider. She gasped and sagged against the doorframe.

Inside the messy room a boy lay on the bed reading a comic book. He looked around the comic, then sat upright. His face was pale and his blue eyes were wide with surprise, then fright.

Wren stepped forward with her hand out to reassure him. "Don't be afraid. I want to talk to you. I want to know if you're all right."

"How'd you get in here?" The boy eased himself to the side of the bed and stood up, looking as if he'd like to run and hide.

"I walked in." She didn't want him to know about the key. "I saw you in the window." And before that, she thought, but she couldn't tell him about that time. "I thought you looked like you were in trouble." She waited, but he didn't say anything. "Are you?"

He shrugged slightly. "Maybe."

"Who are the people living here?"

He tugged on his tee shirt as if it was too tight around his skinny neck. "What do you mean, who are they?"

As Wren moved closer she stepped on a pair of jeans. "You know what I mean. I can't help you unless you talk to me about what's going on here. Why don't you go to school? Why do they leave you here alone when they go away? You're too young to be left alone."

"I'm almost nine!"

She shrugged. "Almost nine. Too young to be left alone."

"I saw you using that camcorder."

"I taped you before you were jerked away from the window."

The boy hiked up his jeans on his thin body. "Yeah, my dad was mad. He said he didn't want anybody to know that I'm here."

His dad! She kept the surprise off her face. "Why is that?"

"He says they could put him in jail for keeping me out of school. He says I can't talk to nobody, or let nobody see me." The boy moved restlessly. "I can't talk to you. I can't let you see me."

"I won't tell anyone at school" Wren touched the wooden footboard of the bed. "What's your name?"

"Billy. Billy Smith."

Smith! Wren stood very still, but her heart almost leaped through her tee shirt. "Where do you live, Billy? I mean, before here."

"125 Green Street. The roof leaked and we had cockroaches."

"Is that why you moved here?"

Billy shook his head. "Dad said we had to for her."

"Your mother."

"She's not my mother. My mother lives in Florida. Jan lives with us and she's trying to decide if she wants to marry Dad. She said she would if he helped her do something. She had to move here to do it."

Wren gripped the footboard tighter. "Did you hear them talk about Mrs. Wheeler? She lived here before you did."

Bill suddenly looked very suspicious. "Maybe I did. Did

you come here to report my dad to the school?"

"I said I wouldn't tell the school. Didn't I say that, Billy?"

"I'm not supposed to trust strangers."

"But I'm not really a stranger. You know that I live right over there. My name is Wren House." She said her whole name without thinking and she saw by his face that he didn't believe it.

"Nobody's named Wren House. "

Wren sighed heavily. "I know, but my mom said that she wanted to name me something everyone would remember once they heard it."

He laughed and suddenly looked like a normal boy instead of a frightened prisoner. "Wren House," he repeated.

"So, you see, I'm not a stranger. I live over there and I came to help you. I don't want anyone to hurt you, or anything." She walked around the end of the bed and stopped just inches from him. "About Mrs. Wheeler."

"She's sick in the hospital."

"Is she your grandma?"

Billy frowned thoughtfully. "Dad and Jan call her grandma sometimes when they talk about her."

"Oh." She had wanted him to say that Mrs. Wheeler wasn't their grandma. Wren looked around the room. "I was in here lots of times to visit Mrs. Wheeler and she always kept the house clean. Did you lose something and try to find it? Everything's so torn apart." She watched Billy closely.

He shook his head. "Jan's always looking for something."

"For money?"

"I don't know. I never asked her. I don't talk to her much." Billy hiked up his jeans again. "I told Dad that I want to go home again. I don't care about the cockroaches or the leak in the roof. I left my toys there. She wouldn't let me bring anything except four comic books."

"Don't you ever get to go outdoors to play?"

He shook his head. "But Dad said once we're ready to leave here, we can move to Texas and buy a nice house and new toys. But if he does that, we have to take Jan."

The front door slammed and Wren clapped her hand over her mouth to push back a terrified scream.

"Billy!" It was the man and he was coming toward the bedroom.

"Help me, Billy," whispered Wren frantically. "I don't want them to know I'm here."

"I sometimes hide in the closet."

The footsteps were closer and Wren knew she'd never make it to the closet. She dropped down and slipped under the bed. Dust tickled her nose and she almost sneezed. She squeezed her nose and breathed through her mouth. Her ears buzzed and she thought she was going to faint with fright. The bed moved and she knew Billy had jumped on it.

"I'm back, Billy."

"Hi, Dad."

Wren heard the quiver in Billy's voice and wondered if his dad did.

"I picked up pop and chips if you want some."

"Maybe later, Dad."

"You're not still mad because Jan slapped you, are you?" The bed moved again and Wren knew the man had sat down. "I told you not to sass her, but you went ahead and did it. She's under a lot of pressure now and we've got to be careful what we say and do around her."

"Can't we leave her and go home by ourselves? Please Dad?"

"No. No, we can't."

The sneeze felt closer and Wren closed her eyes and held her nose even tighter. She dared not sneeze. Silently she prayed for help, for a way out. She knew even under the bed, hiding from possible danger that God was with her.

The bed moved and the man said, "I'm going to the kitchen. Want to come?"

"Is she going to be there?"

"No. She had to run another errand. She'll be back in about an hour."

Wren waited and then she saw Billy's face peeking under the bed.

"Come out, quick! Dad went to the kitchen and you can leave now. Hurry!" Billy's voice came out in a harsh whisper and she knew that he was scared.

"I'll have to go out the front door since your dad could see me if I used the side or back doors." She pushed back her tangled hair.

Billy nodded and motioned for her to follow.

She cleared her throat and crept down the hall after him. What would she do if the man walked out of the kitchen and caught her? Her stomach knotted and she pushed the thought aside.

"Hey, Billy, Did you decide you want something to eat?" Wren ducked into the bathroom and stood with her hand over her hammering heart.

"I'm going to see what's on TV and then I'll be in for a coke." Billy's voice broke. "A coke and potato chips."

"I'm going to fry a hamburger, too. Want one?"

"Sure. I guess."

Wren bit her bottom lip and shivered. Billy stepped into the doorway and motioned for her to follow him. Silently, cautiously, she walked out of the dirty bathroom into the hallway. She followed Billy across the living room. He clicked on the TV and she jumped at the sound.

"Go now," he whispered, pushing her.

"You call me if you need help. I'll try to talk to you again." She wanted to say more, but she didn't dare. She eased open the door and slipped outdoors, closing it with a gentle click, then she ran to her yard. Solving a mystery was not always fun.

8

THE TROUBLEMAKER

Wren reached for the back door of her house, still trembling from her near escape from the Wheeler place. What would she do if Billy changed his mind and told his dad about her?

"I saw what you did, Wren House!"

Wren twirled around to find Paula Gantz standing just a foot away with her hands on her hips and her chin thrust out. She wore yellow jeans and a yellow and white sun top. A gold chain hung around her neck with a small heart dangling from it. Wren's mouth turned bone dry and she couldn't force out a sound. Had Paula really seen her walk out of the neighbor's house. Or was she searching for information?

"I happen to know that the Wheelers are gone and that you just came out of their house. I'm going to tell on you." Paula's brown eyes snapped with excitement and mischief. "You're spoiled rotten and you get by with everything. Well, not this time! You have no business sneaking into that house when nobody's there."

Wren took a deep breath and flipped her hair over her shoulder with the back of her trembling hand. "It just so happens that we have a key to the house and, furthermore, Mr. Wheeler is home now."

"The car is gone!"

"She has it! He's home!"

"I don't believe you, Wren. You're just saying that so you won't get into trouble. You think that I'll go home and forget all about this."

Wren's brain whirled with ideas. She stepped up to Paula and gripped her thin arm. "Let's walk over together and ring the doorbell. When Mr. Wheeler comes to the door, you'll feel stupid. I'll tell him that you thought I was in his house."

Paula jerked away, her face dark with anger. "Oh, all right. So I didn't see you come out, but I saw you at the door."

Wren almost collapsed with relief. "I was just on my way home. I didn't want to bother Mr. Wheeler with his grandma sick." But is wasn't Mr. Wheeler at all. The man was Mr. Smith, Billy's dad. For some terrible reason they called themselves the Wheelers and they were living in Mrs. Wheeler's house. Maybe it was time to talk to Dad and tell him everything. First, though, she'd discuss it with Tim and Bess and then she'd tell Dad.

Paula didn't look totally convinced. "I still might tell

them you were snooping around their place."

Wren shrugged, trying to look like it really didn't matter to her. "Go ahead and tell them." She saw Paula's hesitation and she held her breath until Paula finally turned in a huff and walked away. Wren waited another minute, then dashed across the yards to Bess's house. She found Bess in her bedroom listening to music.

Bess jumped up from the floor. "What's wrong, Wren? I can see by your face that something terrible has happened."

Wren spun around to stare at herself in the full-length mirror on the closet door. She couldn't tell that she looked any different. She turned back to Bess. "I saw the boy. I talked to him."

Bess grabbed her throat. "You did? How? What happened? Tell me before I die!"

Wren collapsed on the chair beside the desk and sucked in her breath. "Not only that, Paula saw me at the Wheeler house and she says she's going to tell!"

"No!" Bess dropped to the edge of the flowered bedspread.

"I talked her out of it for awhile, but I know Paula. She likes to make trouble when she can, especially for me." Wren rubbed her hands up and down her bare arms. "What'll I do?"

"You should stop this whole mystery solving thing and then Paula can't do anything to you."

"But the boy, Bess. What about Billy?"

Bess scooted back on the bed and sat cross-legged with her hands resting on her knees. "Billy?"

"Yes. Billy Smith." Wren told Bess about talking to Billy and of her narrow escape. Bess cried out, turned pale and shook her blonde head.

"I think it's time to talk to Dad about the neighbors. What do you think?"

Bess picked up a stuffed rabbit and hugged it close. "I think you should tell your dad and let him do what he wants to do. I also think you should stay out of it. I know I should."

"I want to talk to Tim first and see what he says. If he agrees, then I might let Dad take charge. I know something strange is going on and I can't let it go without doing something about it."

Bess threw up her arms and rolled her eyes. "Why not, Wren? Do you want to get into serious trouble?"

Wren walked to the window and looked out. Bess's neighbors were swimming in their above-ground pool, splashing and shouting. The sounds drifted through the partly open window. Finally Wren turned back to Bess. "I know Billy needs help. I know Mrs. Wheeler needs help. How can I just forget about them and walk away? It wouldn't be right and you know it. We're doing our video on helping our neighbors, and that help has to be given even when it's the kind of help that Billy and Mrs. Wheeler need. Do you think we should help mow a lawn, but not help an old woman who's in danger?"

Bess pressed her hands to her flushed cheeks and groaned. "Oh, Wren, you always do this to me!"

"Do what?"

"Make me agree with you and go along with you." Bess dropped the rabbit and slid off the bed. "I know Tim will want to solve the mystery no matter what I say, or even what you say. He thinks he's going to be a detective when he grows up."

Wren picked up a yellow pencil and studied it. It felt funny to think that Bess knew something about Tim that she didn't know first. "Did he tell you that?"

"Yes. Last year when you wouldn't talk to him. He said he wanted to get to be friends with you so he could meet your dad and learn stuff from him."

Wren didn't if she should be angry or thankful. "Yes, well, I'll talk to Tim and see what he says about this new development."

"Let's call him."

Wren shook her head. "He said not to. He said to talk to him in school tomorrow."

"But this is important, Wren. He won't care if you call."

She and Bess went out to the hall phone. Bess picked up the phone book and looked for Avery. "He lives on Bond Street and there's A.H. Avery." Bess read out the numbers and Wren dialed it.

Wren licked her dry lips with the tip of her tongue while the phone rang. Was Tim eating his cereal, or was he outdoors playing with friends? On the eleventh ring she hung up and rubbed her damp palms down her jeans. "No one answered. I guess we'll have to wait until tomorrow."

"You could try again later." Bess pushed the phone book back in the drawer. "You know how embarrassing it would be to talk to him in school with everyone around." Bess flushed. "I really didn't mean that the way it sounded."

Wren nodded. She knew just what Bess meant. "If the others knew what a nice guy he is, they might be friendly with him."

"The boys should try harder. I don't think they've been very nice to him."

"They haven't." Wren turned away to hide her guilty expression. She hadn't treated Tim nice at all, either. "I wish the boys would be nice to him first and then maybe the girls would." Maybe she would then, too.

"Did you know his dad doesn't live with him? I heard that his mom is a drunk."

A great sadness for Tim Avery welled up inside Wren and tears stung her eyes. "Tim needs friends, Bess. I am going to be his friend from now on no matter who makes fun of me!"

"Me, too!" Bess nodded firmly. "And I mean it!"

A few minutes later Wren said goodbye and ran home. The woman's car was parked outside the Wheeler garage.

Wren slowed to a walk and stared at the house, wished she could see through the closed curtains. With a troubled sigh, Wren ran to her back door and rushed inside.

"Wren? Come to the den please."

Wren frowned. It was Mom and she sounded very upset. Wren ran down the short hall and stopped in the doorway. Her brothers looked up from playing a video game and Dad laid down the book he was reading. Mom stood beside the small piano. She wore faded jeans and an old shirt of Dad's. "What wrong, Mom?"

"Suppose you tell me, Wren."

Wren shrugged, then froze. Had Paula told something?"

"We just had a visit from Illa Wheeler." Mom stepped toward Wren. "She said that Paula Gantz told her that you have been sneaking around her house, spying. Illa Wheeler is very angry and she said that she wants you to stay out of her yard and away from her house. Well, Wren?"

Philip clicked off the game. He and Neil twisted around to watch Wren.

Wren moved restlessly, her brain whirling. She couldn't outright lie. "Paula is a troublemaker, Mom! You know that!"

"Yes, I do know that. That's why I'm giving you a chance to talk. So, talk. Have you been spying on the Wheelers?"

Wren groaned and looked helplessly at Dad. "There's a mystery, Dad. I was going to tell you all about it soon."

Mom sighed and sank to the edge of the couch. "Oh, Wren."

"You understand, don't you, Dad?"

Dad shot a knowing look at Mom, then walked to Wren and led her to his chair. He sat down and pulled her to the arm of the chair with his arm around her waist. "Wren, it's my job to do detective work. It's not yours. I'm proud of you and of your ability, but you have to learn when to investigate things and when not to."

"We've had this talk before, Wren," said Mom tiredly. "You have promised dozens of times to stop watching people, to stop finding a mystery everywhere you turn."

"I know, Mom." Wren knew it wouldn't do any good to tell Mom that this time she really had found a mystery. "I promise to keep away from Illa Wheeler." She knew the woman calling herself Illa Wheeler was really Jan something-or-other.

"Thank you," said Mom, sounding as if a great weight had lifted off her. "Now, Sam, I think you'd better tell her the latest news."

Wren stiffened as she looked into Dad's face. Her mouth went cotton dry.

"Wren, I called the hospital a while ago to check on Mrs. Wheeler. She had another stroke. She's alive and she's going to be all right, but she's not allowed visitors or phone calls." Dad pulled Wren close.

"I'm sorry, honey."

Wren sniffed back a tear as she wrapped her arms around Dad's neck and held on tight.

9

TIM

Wren and Bess had just reached the school the next day when Wren said, "Bess, I tried to call Tim this morning to tell him to come to school early to meet us, but there wasn't an answer."

Wren hadn't tried to call him last night. She'd been too upset about Mrs. Wheeler, and her parents had taken away her phone privileges for the evening because of what had happened at Mrs. Wheeler's. Wren blinked back sudden tears. Mrs. Wheeler was like a grandmother to her. She'd cross-stitched a picture of a little girl holding an ice cream cone for Wren and framed it so that Wren could hang it on her bedroom wall. Wren had often helped her untangle thread and stretch it across the special bars to keep it straight and separated according to color. How could she turn her back on Mrs. Wheeler when she needed help, even though she didn't know that she did?

"There's Tim now." Bess lifted her arm high and waved. "Hey, Tim!"

Wren saw the heads turn to look at them as they walked toward Tim across the school yard. A cool wind blew back her hair. The gray sky looked as if it would rain soon. They couldn't tape the video without sunlight. But rain wouldn't keep her from her investigation.

"Hi, Tim," Wren said. She smiled and he looked surprised. His red hair was uncombed and he wore the same clothes as yesterday.

"I can meet you after school," he said, darting another look around.

"This is important," said Wren. "I tried to call you."

He frowned. "I told you not to."

"I know, but something happened that I thought you'd want to know." Wren stepped closer and lowered her voice. "I went inside the house."

Someone shouted, "Oh, Tim and Wren. Look at Tim and Wren! They're in love."

Wren's face flamed and she spun around, trying to see who had spoken, but several boys and girls were standing close together, pointing and laughing because she was with Tim. She lifted her chin. "I don't care what any of you say or do, I am going to be his friend."

"Don't do that, Wren," Tim said under his breath, his face as red as his hair.

"Are you going to marry him?" asked David Zimmer.

Wren glared at him. "Jealous, David?"

The others snickered. Two boys nudged David and

mimicked Wren. David pushed them away and they burst out laughing.

"We're going to be friends with Tim," added Bess. "He needs friends. He doesn't have a dad and his mom is a. . . ."

Wren grabbed Bess's arm and jerked her around to silence her. "What's wrong?" Bess looked at Wren in surprise and tried to pull free.

"I do so have a dad," said Tim in a low, tight voice. His face turned gray and he backed away.

"But he doesn't live with you," said Bess.

"Forget all this and listen to me, Tim." Wren frowned at Bess, trying to quiet her before she looked at Tim. She saw the pain in his eyes and she wanted to make it go away, but she didn't know how.

"I do have a dad!" Tim shouted as he turned and ran across the yard and into the school building.

Wren turned on Bess, her brown eyes blazing. "Now, look what you did! Can't you ever watch what you say?"

Bess hung her head. "I'm sorry. But I didn't know Tim would get mad. He knows his dad is gone."

Wren turned to the others. "I think it's time to make friends with Tim Avery. He was here all last year and nobody would be friends with him."

"Not even you, Wren," said Neil, and the others laughed.

Wren flipped back her hair. "I know it and I was wrong."

"I didn't know your sister could be wrong about

anything," said a boy beside Neil.

"Leave her alone." Brian Davies stepped to Wren's side and she went weak all over. "She's right about Tim. It's wrong of us to treat him the way we do. We're supposed to be a Christian school and Christian kids, but we aren't acting like it at all."

Voices buzzed all around. Wren looked up at Brian and whispered, "Thanks." Her heart beat so loud that she was sure he could hear it.

"Why are you blushing, Wren?" asked Paula with a wicked chuckle. "Does Brian know that you love him?"

Wren turned on Paula as anger rushed through her. "Can't you ever leave me alone? I wish you'd stayed in public school where you belong!"

"Don't, Wren." Brian touched her arm and her heart jerked a funny little jerk. "We need to make friends with Paula, too."

"Thanks, Brian," said Paula with a bright smile. "I'll be friends with you any day."

Wren pressed her lips tightly together and locked her hands behind her back.

"Come on, Wren," whispered Bess, tugging on Wren's arm. "We've got to find Tim."

Wren ran with Bess into the school. Only a few students were in the hall. Mr. Abram, the gym teacher, stood in the office doorway talking to someone inside. Wren peeked inside the fifth grade room, but only Miss Brewster was there, standing at the window.

"Maybe he's in the multi-purpose room," whispered Bess.

"Maybe." Wren walked as fast as she could without running. Two boys sat at a corner desk in the multi-purpose room, but Tim wasn't there. Wren's heart sank. If she didn't find him soon she wouldn't be able to talk to him alone until lunch, if then. She always bought her lunch and he carried his in a wrinkled, brown paper bag. He was always just finishing when she reached the table.

Just then she saw him down the hall. She called to him and motioned, but he turned and ran to the boys' restroom, disappearing inside. She sighed heavily and walked back to the fifth grade room. It was almost time for the bell. Maybe she could write a note and sneak it to him during math or reading. She nodded, already planning what she'd say. She'd feel a lot better if she could talk to him, make him understand that she really wanted to be friends and that she needed his help with the mystery.

Several minutes later, after class had started, she peeked at Tim, but he wouldn't turn her way. She listened to Miss Brewster as she pulled out a sheet of lined paper. She wrote, "Tim, I talked to the boy. The people are not who they say they are and we have to do something now. Meet me right after school and we'll make plans."

She folded the note and held it in her palm while she

waited for the perfect time. He sat to her right, but wouldn't turn her way even when she whispered his name. Finally, when Miss Brewster had her back turned to the class as she wrote on the board, Wren leaned over and tossed the note on Tim's desk. She watched as he picked it up and she smiled in relief.

Tim folded the note twice again, then flicked it with his thumb and finger toward Wren. She sagged back and sighed heavily. The note skipped across her desk and hit Paula in the leg. Wren's heart almost stopped.

Paula looked from Wren to Tim, then grinned and picked up the note. Slowly she unfolded it and Wren fumed with anger.

"Give it back," hissed Wren, grabbing for the note.

Paula easily held it out of Wren's reach and Wren didn't dare jump up to get it or Miss Brewster would scold her.

"A note, Paula?" asked Miss Brewster coldly. "Would you like to read it to the class?"

Wren sank lower in her seat and wanted to scream at Paula to give back the note.

Tim looked at Wren and she could see that he was sorry for flicking it.

"I didn't write the note, Miss Brewster," said Paula in a sticky sweet voice. "Wren wrote it, but I'll be glad to read it."

"Please, don't!" The color stained Wren's cheeks, then drained out. "Don't read it."

But Paula was already reading the note to herself and Wren hoped that she wouldn't understand what she was reading.

"Note passing is forbidden and we all know it," said Miss Brewster. "Paula, read the note."

Wren groaned and looked helplessly at Tim. He shrugged and smiled and she felt a little better. Once he heard what she'd written, maybe he'd know how badly she needed to talk to him.

Paula cleared her throat and read in a loud voice, "Dear Tim, I love you. Do you love me? Meet me after school and we'll make plans."

Wren gasped and shook her head. Helplessly she looked at Tim and she saw his embarrassment as the class snickered and laughed. "I didn't write that!" cried Wren.

"You didn't write the note, Wren?" asked Miss Brewster coldly.

"Yes, I wrote the note, but I didn't write what she read! I didn't!" Wren grabbed for the note, but Paula tore it into pieces and ran for the wastebasket. She dropped it inside triumphantly, then walked back to her seat.

"That was not necessary, Paula," said Miss Brewster. "Wren, you will write fifty lines saying, 'I will not write notes in school.' Hand them in in the morning." She walked around her desk. "Now, let's continue with our math lesson."

Wren looked helplessly at Tim, but once again he

wouldn't look at her. Automatically she did her work and waited impatiently for the school day to end. A chilly rain beat against the windows and she hated to think of walking home. Maybe Dad would pick them up.

Just as the bell rang she jumped up and grabbed Tim's arm before he could leave. He glared at her, but she wouldn't turn loose. "The note said that I talked to the boy and the people living in the Wheeler house aren't who they say they are."

"Who cares? I don't! It's your mystery now!"

"Why? I want to be friends!"

"Only because you feel sorry for me." Jerking free, Tim ran from the room and she let him go.

Tears stung Wren's eyes and she ducked her head as she walked to the hall for her raincoat.

10

THE LOCK BOX

Wren walked listlessly through the quiet house. Dad had dropped her and Neil off, then driven away to a meeting with a client. Philip had a guitar lesson and Dad said he'd see that he got home afterward.

In the kitchen Wren poured herself a glass of orange juice and drank it. What could she do without either Bess or Tim? She stood at the window and looked out at the Wheeler place. The car stood outside the garage and a light glowed from the front window. What was happening inside that house? She turned at a sound behind her. Neil stood in the doorway looking at her. He'd changed into gray sweats.

"I heard you got into trouble again today, this time for writing a note." Neil shook his head. "When will you learn, Wren?"

"Paula made it worse. She made up a love note and read it like I wrote it, but I didn't. I only wanted to tell Tim about something." She almost told him what the note had said and then she remembered that she wasn't supposed to do any more investigating.

Neil pulled out the crackers and peanut butter. "I didn't think you'd write a love note." His voice cracked and he looked pleased with himself. He spread peanut butter on several crackers, arranged them on a small flowered plate and carried them to the table. He poured himself a glass of milk, then sat down.

Wren walked around the kitchen, her mind whirling. Finally she pulled out a chair and sat across the table from Neil. His mouth was full of cracker and peanut butter. She watched him chew for a minute. "I wonder if Mrs. Wheeler had diamond rings or money or any other valuables."

Neil swallowed and gulped down some milk. He rubbed his hand across his mouth and reached for another cracker. "She had something important."

Wren sat very still and tried not to act too excited. If Neil suspected why she was asking, he wouldn't answer her. "How do you know?"

"I was here when she gave Mom the lock box."

"The lock box?" Shivers dashed up and down Wren's spine and she had to sit on her hands to keep them quiet.

Neil pushed another cracker into his mouth and it seemed like the whole month of September passed while Wren waited for him to speak again. "It's a sturdy plastic box about this big." He measured about twelve inches by twelve inches with his hands. "Mrs. Wheeler brought it over one Saturday afternoon about two weeks before she went to the hospital. Mom said maybe Mrs. Wheeler had a premonition that something was going to happen to her. She said she wanted Mom to keep it for her until she could get it to a safety deposit box at the bank." Neil leaned back and narrowed his blue eyes. "For some reason she didn't want to leave it at her place. She said too many old women had their stuff stolen from them and she didn't want her stuff taken."

"Do you know what kind of stuff?" Wren's voice cracked and she bit back a nervous giggle.

"I didn't stay around to listen. Mom said she'd keep it in her bedroom in a safe spot and I left." Neil pushed another cracker in his mouth.

Wren eased herself up. She had to have a look at the lock box, but she dare not let Neil suspect. He wouldn't approve at all. He'd say that she was going to get into trouble again, then remind her that she was in enough trouble already.

A few minutes later she stood inside her parents' bedroom with the door closed. The lavender, blue and white of the room always made her feel cheerful. She walked across the plush blue carpet to the closet where she knew her mom often kept important things. Wren's stomach knotted and her hand trembled as she opened the closet. She found the lock box in the far corner behind a boot box. Slowly she pulled it out and rubbed her hands over it.

"I wish Tim was here right now," she whispered to the empty room. She turned the box over and gasped. A small key was taped to the bottom of it. Dare she open it and peek inside? She rubbed the tape and felt the outline of the tiny key.

She closed her eyes and took a deep breath. Then slowly, carefully, she pulled back the tape. She lifted off the key and held it. Perspiration popped out on her forehead. Rain beat against the window.

"This is terrible," she whispered as she unsteadily pushed the key in the lock. But she had to look inside the box to make sure the people at the Wheeler house had a strong enough motive to pass themselves off as relatives.

The key turned easily and she lifted up the lid. Inside she saw papers, a folder filled with old coins, a few photos and a small chest. She lifted out the small wooden box and opened the lid. Inside, nestled on a piece of royal blue velvet, were five rings that looked very beautiful and very expensive. One at a time she picked them up and studied them. She touched the ruby and diamonds, the emerald, the pearl. She slipped the square cut diamond on her finger and held it up, then hastily slipped it off and put it back in place. From what she'd heard Mom say about the price of jewels, Wren knew the rings were worth a lot of money.

Carefully she put the box back and as she did she saw an envelope full of money. Her hand shook as she lifted out the envelope and counted out the bills, $2000 in twenties. "Wow!" She pushed the money back in place and said it again. She knew there was a lot money involved here, money enough for a motive.

She pulled out the photos and looked at pictures of Mrs. Wheeler as a bride, one of both the bride and groom, Mrs. Wheeler holding a baby boy, and the boy alone. The very last picture was one that Wren hadn't seen before. It was a man about Dad's age and an older man. Wren turned over the picture and her eyes widened. "Jeff and Aaron. Son and Grandson." Wren blew out her breath. Here was solid proof that the man next door was not Jeff Wheeler.

"I have to show this stuff to Tim and see what he says!" She jumped up and ran to the phone beside the bed. She dialed Tim's number and waited breathlessly. There was no answer and she hung up with a clatter. Somehow she had to get in touch with Tim and tell him the latest. Together they could decide what to do.

She locked the box and retaped the key. At the closet door she hesitated. If she put it back and needed it when Mom was home, she wouldn't be able to get it. She'd have to put it somewhere else. She'd have to put it in her room until she could talk to Tim. After that she'd show it to Dad no matter how angry he got.

In her bedroom she pulled the desk chair across the floor to her closet. She pushed the box back in the corner of her shelf and set a shoe box in front of it. She piled things neatly on and around it so that if anyone looked in her closet they wouldn't see the box.

Her legs trembled as she put the chair back in place then collapsed on it. If Dad was home right now, she'd run to him and tell him everything. She'd show him the proof that she'd found no matter how upset he got at first. Once he heard her story and saw the proof, he'd get over his anger and help her. But he wasn't home. Mom wasn't home either, but even if she was, Wren knew she wouldn't give her a chance to talk. As a lawyer, Mom always did everything according to the rules. Looking into the locked box was definitely breaking a rule, maybe more than one.

Wren walked to her bed and ran her hand over the pink and yellow spread as she wrinkled her forehead in thought. Should she talk to Neil? She shook her head. Neil would never listen or agree with her about anything.

She ran to the kitchen and peeked inside. Neil wasn't there. She hurried to the phone and dialed Tim's number again. It rang and rang, but there was still no answer. With a ragged sigh she hung up and turned to look out the window. The rain had stopped and a weak sun shone through the clouds. Should she ride her bike to Tim's house and talk to him?

The phone jangled and she jumped and laughed, suddenly very nervous. She reached to answer the phone and a strange feeling washed over her.

11

FRANTIC CALL

Wren held the phone to her ear. "Hello?" She sounded uncertain and that upset her. What was wrong with her? Were all the happenings getting to her?

"Wren?" The voice was squeaky. "Wren House?"

"Yes." Was it someone calling to tease her about her name? That had happened a lot of times in the last few years.

"I couldn't remember your name and I tried and tried and I saw a bird out the window and remembered.

"She frowned impatiently. "Who is this?"

"It's me. Billy. Billy Smith."

She gripped the receiver so hard her fingers ached. "Billy! Is something wrong? Do you need help?"

"She's mad at Dad and she yelled at him and hit him." Billy's words were full of tears and Wren had to listen carefully to hear him.

"Did she hurt you, Billy?"

"Not yet, but she said she would if Dad won't do what she wants."

"What does she want, Billy?"

"I don't know! They were yelling about that lady they sometimes call Grandma. Jan says Dad needs to go see that lady and do something to her, but Dad says he won't. He wants to leave here, and I do, too!" Billy's voice ended in a wail.

"Are you home all alone right now?" Wren stretched her neck to see the Wheeler house from where she stood. She couldn't see the garage at all.

"Yes, but they'll be back right away."

"Shall I come get you and bring you to my house?" Oh, dare she do that?

"What about my dad?" Billy sounded frantic, close to hysteria.

"I'll tell him where you are as soon as he gets back. And I'll do it without her hearing me." Nervous perspiration soaked Wren's body and the receiver was slippery in her hand. "You ham up, Billy, and wait for me by the side door. Will you?"

"I will," he said, sniffing back a sob.

Just then she caught a movement outdoors. "Wait! Don't hang up yet, Billy! I see your dad and her walking to the house. I can't get you now, but I will soon. I promise! Hang up and don't let them know you called me. Hang up right now, Billy!" She waited until she heard the click, then she hung up and ran to the window. Her breathing sounded loud in the quiet kitchen. She watched as the man and woman walked into the house, closing the door after them. Would Billy tell them he'd called her? She shivered and wrapped her arms around herself, rocking back and forth.

The phone rang. She jumped and cried out, then dashed to answer it. When she heard her mother's voice on the other end, she sagged in relief.

"Wren, I won't be home until about seven. Tell the others, and go ahead and eat without me."

"Okay. See you later, Mom.

"Wren?"

"Yes?"

"You sound funny. Is everything all right?"

Wren hesitated. She desperately wanted to tell someone about Billy's call, but she knew she couldn't tell Mom. "Everything's fine, Mom. Don't worry about dinner. We'll manage alone."

"I know, but I'll miss you. Dinner's a special time for me, a time when I get to be with my wonderful family."

The words wrapped around Wren's heart and she smiled. Sometimes she thought her mom liked her career more than her family. "We'll wait and have dessert with you."

"That's wonderful. Bye, sweetheart. See you later."

"Bye, Mom." Wren stood beside the phone for a long time, thinking. Mom had been a lawyer for three years now. Dad had been a detective for as long as she could remember. It would be strange if it were any different. It would be terrible if she had to live the way Tim did. Or Billy.

Once again she tried calling Tim, but still there was no answer. She had to talk to him. He would know what to do.

She ran to Neil's room and knocked on his door, then peeked inside. He turned from his computer with a frown. "Mom won't be home until seven. She said we're to eat without her. I have to go out for awhile. See you later." She closed the door and ran before he could ask her what she was going to do.

In the den she rummaged around in the desk drawer until she found the Jordan city map. She spread it out and found Bond Street. It would be easy enough to find his house. Before she folded up the map she hunted for Green Street. Billy had said that they'd lived on Green Street. It wasn't far from Bond. Maybe she and Tim could check it out. She folded the map and stuffed it back in the drawer. Hopefully it wouldn't start raining again.

Just as she reached the back door, someone knocked on it. It was probably Bess. Maybe she'd got home early and decided to come over. Wren opened the door, then bit back a startled cry. The woman who called herself Illa Wheeler stood there. She wore white slacks and a yellow knit shirt with a round neckline. Her hair was held back on both sides with wide brown combs. She didn't smile and neither did Wren.

"Is your mother home, little girl?"

"No."

"Your father?"

"No." Wren started to close the door, but the woman stuck out her hand and stopped her.

"Maybe you can help me."

"I don't think I can."

"But you never can tell, can you?" The woman rubbed her hand across her arm. "It just occurred to us that Grandma might have left something here with you folks when she went to the hospital."

Wren kept her face blank and tried to stand still. Butterflies fluttered wildly in her stomach as she waited for the woman to continue.

"Did she?"

"Did she what?" asked Wren, playing her dumb act that she sometimes used on her brothers to make them mad.

"Leave anything of hers here?" The woman's face turned red and her eyes darkened with impatience.

"She gave us a bouquet of her flowers once. Is that what you mean?"

The woman looked as if she wanted to scream and Wren forced back a giggle. "No! That is not what I mean! Did she bring over any important papers or . . . or valuables?"

Wren frowned and pretended to think very carefully.

"I never saw your grandma bring anything like that here."

"Oh, what do you know? I'll ask your mother when she returns. When will that be?"

Wren panicked, but she wouldn't let it show. "She won't be home until late. She just called and told me."

The woman doubled her fists and muttered under her breath. "What about your dad?"

"I don't know about him. He's a private detective, you know. He catches criminals all the time and hands them over to the police. Did you know that? He has a keen eye and a sharp nose for dirty work." She'd heard many people say that about her dad and she loved to repeat it, especially now. The look on the woman's face made Wren want to whoop with laughter. "If you ever know of anybody doing anything against the law, just call my dad and he'll catch them red-handed."

"When will he be home?" The words were sharp with impatience.

"I can't say. He's working on an important case right now, and I really don't know when he'll be home. Should I send him over to your house when he gets here?"

"No! That won't be necessary." The woman turned on her heels and practically ran to the Wheeler house.

Wren closed the door, covered her mouth and giggled. Then she thought about what would happen if that woman came over when Mom was home. Mom just might decide to give the lock box to her. Wren's eyes widened and she moaned. She had to act fast so that Mom wouldn't want to give the lock box to the stranger.

She wheeled her ten-speed out of the garage and rode away. Cool wind whipped her hair back. Puddles of water stood here and there and splashed up on her leg as she rode through them. Cars whizzed past, spraying water on her. She shivered against the chill of it.

Finally she turned onto Bond Street. The houses were run down and close together with tiny, weed-infested lawns. She stopped at 210 Bond Street and leaned against her bike as she stared at it. The sidewalk that led up to the front step was cracked and weeds sprouted through the cracks. She would hate to live in such a place. Tim probably did, too.

Carefully she stood her bike in the small yard and walked up to the scarred front door. She tugged her lavender sweatshirt down over her jeans, then knocked as hard as she could. It hurt her knuckles and she winced as she rubbed them against her shirt.

The door opened and Tim stood there. His mouth dropped open, then he slammed the door shut in her face.

She backed up, staring at the closed door as her eyes slowly filled with scalding tears.

12

DETECTIVE WORK

Wren walked slowly to her ten-speed, then stopped and lifted her head. She had to talk to Tim. She had to! She blinked away her tears and turned back to the house. Once again she knocked. Tim didn't answer and she knocked again. "Open this door right now, Tim Avery!"

"Go away, Wren! I don't want to talk to you."

"I know you don't, but this is important. I need your help right now. On business. Detective business." She waited, her hands at her sides, her feet apart. "DETECTIVE BUSINESS!"

The door inched open and Tim poked his face out. "Yeah?"

She nodded. "Tim, we have to forget that terrible business at school and get on with our mystery. Will you help me? Please? I need your head for deductive reasoning."

"You do?" Tim smiled and it lit up his face. He stepped out and closed the door. "You won't talk any more about me not having a dad?"

"Not at all. Unless you want to talk. I came to tell you about a phone call from Bill and a locked box and a visit from that woman that calls herself Illa Wheeler."

"Let's go around back and sit down where we can talk."

"We don't have time, Tim. Get your bike and let's ride!"

He looked toward the house, shrugged and then ran around the house. A minute later he came back with the new ten-speed.

They walked their bikes along as Wren told him all that had happened. "So, our first stop will be 125 Green Street and we'll ask about the Smiths." They hopped on their bikes and rode fast. A cloud covered the weak sun and it looked as if it would rain again. They stopped twice at red lights, then turned onto Green Street. It looked much like Bond Street. Kids ran around laughing and shouting. Finally they found 125 and stopped, standing with their bikes.

"It's in bad shape," said Tim, looking at the house.

Wren agreed. This house looked even worse than Tim's. "It looks empty."

"We'll knock anyway." Tim laid his bike down and ran lightly to the front door. A piece of wood was nailed over a section of the broken glass in the door.

Wren watched Tim knock, then look around before he knocked again.

A man on the porch of the house next door called, "No use to knock. Smiths aren't home. Haven't been for a couple of days now."

Tim ran to Wren and they walked to the neighbor.

"We're looking for Billy. He's eight. Light brown hair and blue eyes. Is that Billy's house?"

The man nodded. "Yup. Billy. Lives with his dad George. A woman moved in with them a while back. Works as some kind of nurse at the hospital. An LPN. That's it. But they aren't here now."

Wren shot Tim an exultant look before she turned back to the gray haired man. "Is the woman's name Jan? Jan . . . " Wren wrinkled her forehead in thought as she studied the man.

"Jan Bliss. Sharp-tongued woman. Billy don't like her much at all. Don't blame him a bit. I don't like her myself. She trampled my flowers and as you can see I only have a few."

Wren looked at the scraggly row of marigolds. Right then she decided to bring the man a giant bouquet of flowers. "I'm Wren and this is Tim." She didn't want to go through the whole deal of telling her last name.

"Glad to meet you both. I'm Amos Pike. Lived her most of my life, I have. Smiths lived right there since Billy was no bigger than a hop toad. I don't know where they could've got to. They didn't say anything about moving."

"Thanks for all of your help, Mr. Pike," said Wren.

"I'll tell them you were looking for 'em when they come back. If they come back." Amos rubbed a weathered hand across his wrinkled face. "They never did get much company. But I don't neither. Not much at all."

"We'll come see you again," said Tim, smiling.

"You don't have to tell the Smiths about us stopping by. We want to . . . surprise them." Wren moved restlessly. She hated to leave the lonely man, but she knew they had to get on with things. The first thing now would be to talk to Dad, now that they had proof and a motive for commiting a crime.

Mr. Pike, how would you like to be in a movie?" Tim asked as he stood with his hands on his thin hips and a grin on his freckled face.

Mr. Pike chuckled. "Well. Well. What's this about?"

"We're making a movie for a school project, and we'd like you to be in it." Tim glanced at Wren and she nodded, glad that he'd thought of it. "If it's sunny tomorrow after school, we'll be here. If it's all right with you."

He smoothed back his gray hair and grinned. "Sure. It's fine with me. I've never been in a movie. Imagine that. Me in a movie."

"We'll probably see you tomorrow then," said Wren. She walked to her bike with Tim and they waved and rode away.

"Where to now?" asked Tim.

"The hospital. I'm afraid for Mrs. Wheeler."

They rode in silence side by side down Green Street. Finally Wren said, "I'm sorry for the way I treated you last year, Tim."

He flushed. "Aw, forget it, Wren."

"I can't! I was rotten to you."

"Yeah, you were." Tim grinned and she knew she was forgiven.

"I sure didn't act the way Jesus wanted me to."

"It's not always easy to. I know." Tim's face was set and he looked away.

"Are you thinking about your dad?"

Tim shook his head. "My mom. Bess was right, you know. She is an alcoholic. I've tried to get her to stop drinking, but she won't."

"I'm sorry, Tim." Wren wanted to reach over and touch him, but she didn't.

"I keep the phone turned off so that if someone calls me, she won't answer and embarrass me."

"So that's why I could never get you!"

"I didn't want you to know about her. We were just getting to be friends and I thought it might make you turn against me."

Wren gripped her handlebars tighter. He would probably have been right earlier, but not any longer. "We'll be friends no matter what, Tim."

He grinned and looked more like his cheerful self. Let's get to the hospital." He leaned forward and pedaled hard. Wren fell in behind him.

At the hospital they rode the elevator to the fourth floor. Wren took a deep breath and glanced at Tim.

"We have to be very careful, Tim. If Jan Bliss is here, we can't let her see us."

Tim nodded.

They walked to the nurse's station and the dark haired nurse turned and looked at them with a wide smile.

"Hi, kids. What can I do for you?"

"Is Jan Bliss working now?" asked Wren.

"Not at present. She was here earlier. You friends of hers?"

Wren shook her head. "We just wanted to see her, but we can find her at home, I guess."

"Does she still live on Green Street?" asked Tim.

The nurse frowned thoughtfully. "You know, I heard her talk about moving, but I can't remember where to."

Wren moved from one foot to the other. "Could it have been Lyons Street?"

"Yes! Yes, I believe it was!"

They talked a few more minutes, then were interrupted by the phone and another nurse. Wren and Tim walked away from the desk, then slipped into Mrs. Wheeler's room.

Wren pressed her hand to her heart as she crept to the side of the bed. Mrs. Wheeler looked as if she'd break easily and as if she'd shrunken. Her nose looked much too large for her thin face. Wren looked closer, then turned to Tim with wide, frightened eyes. "That's not Mrs. Wheeler," she whispered.

"Then who is it?"

Wren backed away, suddenly very frightened. "What have they done with Mrs. Wheeler?" Wren gripped Tim's arm. "Could she be . . . dead?"

"Let's go ask." He eased out of the room, then motioned for her to follow when the coast was clear. They walked back to the same nurse that they had talked to before. She looked at them with raised eyebrows.

"I thought you two left."

Wren licked her dry lips. The hospital smells suddenly made her stomach sick. "Mrs. Wheeler is a good friend of mine and my neighbor. Could you tell me what room she's in?"

The nurse flipped through the list. "Room 408."

Wren reached blindly for Tim's hand and gripped it. "Is she going to be all right?"

"She had a pretty bad time, but she's just fine now."

"Can we go see her?" asked Tim. "We just want to peek in and make sure she's all right."

The nurse hesitated, then nodded. "Just peek in, remember. You can't stay in with her and tire her out. Poor thing never has visitors."

Wren blinked back tears as she walked beside Tim down the hallway. She stopped in the doorway of Room

408 and looked toward the bed just as Mrs. Wheeler turned her head.

"Wren," she said weakly. Then she smiled. "Hello, Wren." Her voice was stronger and Wren smiled.

"Hello, Mrs. Wheeler. This is my friend Tim Avery."

"Hello, Tim." He grinned. "Hi."

"When will you come home?" asked Wren.

"Soon I hope."

"I hope so, too!" Wren ran to her and kissed the soft, wrinkled cheek. "The nurse said we couldn't stay, so we have to leave now. I'm glad you're better."

"Did your grandson and his wife visit you today?" asked Tim.

Mrs. Wheeler frowned. "Every time they come, I'm asleep."

"We'll tell the nurse to wake you up next time," said Wren.

"You do that. I've tried, but they won't listen to me."

"We must go now," said Tim, tugging on Wren's arm.

"I know. Bye, Mrs. Wheeler. I'll be glad when you're home again. I miss you a lot."

She smiled weakly, and Wren and Tim walked out. In the elevator Tim said, "Well, she doesn't even know that her grandson isn't here. Jan Bliss probably tells her that they come to visit while she was asleep."

"The other nurse said that Mrs. Wheeler never has visitors," said Wren. "I bet it was all Jan Bliss's idea to tell

Mom and Dad that Mrs. Wheeler couldn't see anyone! I can't wait to break this case wide open."

Tim nodded.

Wren glanced at her watch. "Dad should be home now. Our next step is to talk to him."

13

A TERRIBLE SURPRISE

Wren stopped short, just inside the back door and Tim bumped into her. "Mom! I thought you said you'd be gone until seven."

Mom turned from loading the washer. "Hi, Wren. Tim. I didn't have to stay over after all." She wore old jeans and a sweatshirt and the room smelled like laundry soap.

Wren closed the door after Tim. "Is Dad home? We have to talk to him."

Mom shook her head. "He's not here yet. Would I do?"

Wren looked at Tim and he shrugged. Dare she tell Mom? "It's about . . . about the neighbors."

Mom frowned. "Then don't start, Wren! I mean it! I do not want to listen to another person complain to me about you."

"It's different this time, Mom. This time I have proof! I know that those people aren't who they say they are."

"Oh, Wren," Mom said tiredly, shaking her head.

"Spare me, please. I've had a long, hard day."

Just then someone knocked on the back door and Wren rushed to answer it, sure it was Bess. But it was Jan Bliss and she looked past Wren to Mom.

"Mrs. House, I need to speak to you."

Wren shot a look at Tim. What could they do now?

Lorrene House smiled and pushed back her hair. "Hello, Mrs. Wheeler." She darted a warning look at Wren. "Come into the den. Do you have time for a cup of tea?"

"No. Thanks anyway." Jan Bliss walked after Lorrene and Wren wanted to shout out the truth.

"Come on, Tim," Wren whispered, motioning to him as she crept after Mom and Jan. "We can't let her talk Mom out of Mrs. Wheeler's things."

They stayed outside the den and stood against the wall listening. The door was open and it was easy to hear.

"Mrs. House, I talked to Grandma and she said she left something with you. I think she'd feel a lot better if you gave it to me to keep for her."

"But she didn't say anything about giving it to you."

Wren grinned. Good for Mom.

"I'm sure if you could speak to her now, she'd want you to give it to me. She always wanted me to have her rings, you know. She says it would please her to see them on my fingers when I visit her next."

"Well, maybe you're right. You are her relative and I'm

only a neighbor."

Wren turned frantically to Tim. "What now?" she mouthed.

"That's right," said Jan. "I do appreciate your understanding."

"Wren," called Lorrene. "Come here, please."

Wren slapped her hand to her heart. How could this be happening? Everything had been going along so well, and now this!

"Wren will bring the box and you can take it home," Lorrene said. "Wren! Maybe she stepped out. I'll go get it myself. Excuse me, please."

Wren dashed into the room. "Did you call, Mom?"

"Yes. Mrs. Wheeler wants her grandmother's lock box. I put it in my bedroom. It's where I usually hide your Christmas presents. You know where." Mom grinned and Wren nodded. "Bring it to me, please."

Wren nodded and walked back out, then dashed to her bedroom with Tim on her heels. She scrambled up on the chair and frantically pulled things away until she reached the lock box. She pulled the key off the bottom as she jumped off the chair.

"What're you doing, Wren?"

"We can't let her take this stuff! She'll take it and disappear and no one will be able to find her." Wren opened the box, grabbed an empty shoe box and dumped the things into it. Then she closed and locked the box, dropping the key into her shoe box. Her heart thudded and suddenly she felt hot. "Mom won't like this at all, Tim."

"She'll get over her anger when she learns the truth."

"I hope so." Wren pushed the shoe box to the back of her closet and dropped a sweater over it.

"Doesn't the box feel empty?" Tim took it and shook it.

"You're right!" Wren looked around. She gathered up several pages of blank lined paper, a couple of rocks that she'd picked up in South Dakota and two pencils. She unlocked the box again, filled it with her things, locked it and dropped the key back in her shoe box. "We're ready." Her mouth was so dry it was hard to talk.

A minute later she held the lock box out to Mom. "Tim and I are going outdoors for awhile."

"Fine." Lorrene held the box out to Jan, then pulled it to her and lifted it so she could see the bottom.

"What's wrong?" asked Jan suspiciously.

Wren stopped at the door. She wanted to hear this.

"The key is gone. Mrs. Wheeler taped it to the bottom of the box so that she wouldn't lose it, but it's gone now. Wren, run to the bedroom and see if it fell off."

"Wait!" Jan reached for the box. "I'm sure she has another key. Don't trouble yourself. I am in a hurry."

Lorrene hesitated, then held the box out to her. Jan took it with a quick thank you and rushed out. A minute later the back door slammed.

Wren took a deep breath. "Mom, I have proof that that woman is not Illa Wheeler."

"What?" Lorrene's voice crack. "This is no time to joke, Wren!"

"She's right, Mrs. House," said Tim, nodding his red head, a serious look on his face.

Lorrene shoved her fingers through her hair. "Don't do this to me kids. I can't take it."

Wren touched Mom's arm. "Listen, Mom. That woman is Jan Bliss, an LPN at the hospital. She found things out from Mrs. Wheeler and is trying to steal her things."

"What's this I hear?" Sam House walked into the room and looked from one to another.

"Wren's trying to tell me that woman is an LPN out to steal from Mrs. Wheeler." Lorrene caught Sam's large hand and clung to it. "You said you'd deal with this, Sam, and she's still doing it."

He pulled free and slipped an arm around his wife. "We can at least listen to her, Lorrene. I've been working on a similar case. Sick old people check into the hospital and the next thing you know their valuables are stolen from their homes. It happens." He turned to Wren. "What do you know about this woman, Wren?"

"Promise you won't get mad." Wren stood behind a chair with her hands gripping the back of it.

"We'll listen carefully." Dad smiled at her and she relaxed a little."I can't take two detectives in one house," said Mom. She sank to the couch and locked her hands around her knees.

"I know that the woman is Jan Bliss," said Wren. As quickly as she could, she and Tim told all that they knew. "We were going to tell you everything and show you our proof, Dad, but you weren't home."

"Sorry about that. Where is the proof?"

"It was in the lock box." Wren looked at Mom and quickly away.

Lorrene gasped. "In the lock box? But I just gave it to that woman! Now you don't have any proof!"

Wren grinned and Tim chuckled. "I'll be right back." She ran to her room for the shoe box and held it out to Dad. She showed him the picture of Mrs. Wheeler's son and grandson. "That man over in the Wheeler house is George Smith and he doesn't look anything like this."

Lorrene peeked through the stuff in the box. "I shouldn't be doing this, you know. I really shouldn't."

"It's time to call the police." Wren's dad said. "I'll give Mick a call."

The front doorbell rang and Wren jumped, then laughed. She didn't have anything to worry about now. The case was solved. She wasn't in danger at all.

"Go answer it, Wren," said Mom.

"Come with me, Tim." Wren ran to the front door with Tim close behind her. She pulled open the door to find Paula Gantz standing there. Wren wanted to slam it shut.

"Hello, Wren," said Paula with a fake smile. "Hello, Tim. Can I come in for awhile?" She walked right in and closed the door.

"We're busy," said Wren.

"I guess with the neighbors leaving you won't have anyone else to spy on, will you, Wren?" Paula jerked open the door and Wren grabbed her arm before she could leave.

"What're you talking about?"

Paula pried Wren's fingers loose. "The Wheelers are packing things into a trailer and are leaving."

"Tell Dad, Tim," shouted Wren. She pushed past a surprised Paula and raced around the house to the Wheeler place. Somehow she had to stop them. Could she stop them in time?

14

WREN TO THE RESCUE

Wren stopped in the Wheeler yard and cupped her hands around her mouth. "Billy! Billy Smith, can you come out to play?" She waited a minute, then ran to the door, knocked and rang the doorbell. "Billy Smith! We went to see Amos Pike."

The door burst open and Jan Bliss stood there, her face dark with anger. "Get away from here right now before I call the police on you!"

"I came to play with Billy."

"I'm in here, Wren," called Billy from inside the house. "She won't let me come out."

Jan grabbed Wren and jerked her into the house. "You think you're smart, don't you, little girl? Well, you aren't! We got what we came for and we're leaving now."

George Smith walked out of the kitchen, his face damp with perspiration. "Let the girl go right now, Jan. We're in enough trouble already."

"You sure are," said Wren. "I know that you're Jan Bliss

and you're George Smith. Your son is Billy and he's eight years old. You're trying to steal valuables from Mrs. Wheeler because she's in the hospital and helpless."

"I'm getting out of here!" cried Jan. She grabbed the lock box and headed for the door.

"I emptied the stuff out of that," said Wren, pointing to the box. "I put my paper and some rocks and pencils in it."

"What?" Jan's voice rose and almost choked her. "You did what?" She flung the box from her and leaped at Wren. Wren jumped back into George Smith. His rough hands closed around her arms and her heart sank. Frantically she looked toward the door. Where were Dad and the police?

"Leave her alone, Jan. She's just a kid."

Jan grabbed for Wren, but George pushed her behind him and she peeked out at the angry woman. The doorbell rang.

"Open up. This is the police!"

Jan gasped and the color drained from her face. She rushed past George trying to go out the back door. She jerked open the door and Sam House stood there, blocking her way.

"Going somewhere, Mrs. Bliss?" He pulled her into the front room and handed her over to the police officer, then he turned to Wren. "Are you all right?"

She nodded and moved close to him, suddenly feeling very weak.

Tim stood in the doorway with nosy Paula Gantz behind him. Wren waited until the policeman took George and Jan and Billy away. Billy waved to her and she waved back, then ran outdoors.

"Thanks, Paula," Wren said with a giggle.

Paula looked blank. "For what?"

"You'd make a good detective, Paula," said Tim.

She backed away., her face red. "Are you making fun of me or something?"

"Not at all," said Wren. "If it hadn't been for you knowing what was going on here and telling us, they might have gotten away with a crime. You helped stop them."

"I did?" Paula looked pleased with herself, then looked around to see who she could tell. She saw Bess walk out her back door. "Bess! Guess what?"

Dad put his around around Wren. "I'm going to help Mick wind things up here and then we'll be over to get Mrs. Wheeler's valuables. They're going to the bank first thing in the morning." He hugged Wren close, and she smelled his aftershave. "You both did an excellent job, kids. Wren, we're going to have to talk later about some of the things you've done, but I want you to know I'm proud of you, both of you. You're good detectives."

Wren nodded, knowing her dad would be fair, but she couldn't help swelling with pride at his praise. She saw that Tim was just as proud. She watched Dad walk back into the

Wheeler house, and then she turned to Tim and laughed triumphantly. He threw back his head and laughed with her.

"The mystery is solved," said Wren softly.

Tim nodded. "The mystery is solved."

"Tomorrow we go back to our ordinary lives. You and Bess and I will have to make our movie for school. I know we'll get a good grade on it."

"It'll be fun to film Mr. Pike. I might stop and see him on my way home." Tim stuck his fingers in his back pockets and cocked his head. "I think he needs a friend."

"I think so, too." Wren smiled at Tim. She wanted to say so much about friendship, but the right words wouldn't come to mind, so she didn't say anything. "Let's go tell Bess about our adventure before you have to go home."

"I think we'll be talking about this for a long time."

"Me, too. Until another mystery comes along for us to solve." Wren grinned at Tim and he grinned back as they ran toward Bess's yard.

Project Cockroach

"We'll go down in Jefferson School history."

That's what Ben Anderson promises when he gets Josh to agree to his plan. And turning loose a horde of cockroaches in Mrs. Bannister's desk drawer does sound impressive. Josh knows what Wendell, his peculiar next-door neighboor and classmate, would say, but what would you expect from a kid who actually goes to the library in the summertime?

Josh's mom wants him to be a good student and stay out of trouble. His long-distance dad back in Woodview wants him to "have a good year." Wendell wants him to go to church. But Josh isn't sure that even God can help him find answers to the questions in his life. He just wants to make a few friends and fit into his new world . . . even if it means taking a risk or two.

ELAINE K. McEWAN, an elementary school principal and the mother of two grown children, knows a lot of kids like Josh.

Chariot Books™
David C. Cook Publishing Co.

The Best Defense

"You sure know how to make a mother worry."

Josh has lived in Grandville barely two months, and he's already met the paramedics, the police, some teenaged would-be thugs, and a long-haired leather worker named Sonny. No wonder his mom gets a little anxious from time to time.

Josh thinks karate lessons would take care of some of his worries, but they aren't likely to help his relationship with Samantha Sullivan, the bossiest kid in the fifth grade. And they won't make his dad call more often.

Sonny tells him the key to conquering his fear is prayer . . . but Josh isn't sure that prayer is the answer. He needs to explore the possiblility. What if it doesn't work in a dark tunnel when he's facing two thugs?

ELAINE K. McEWAN, an elementary school principal and the mother of two grown children, knows a lot of kids like Josh.

Chariot Books™
David C. Cook Publishing Co.

Adam Straight and the Mysterious Neighbor

Listen to the "Spider Lady"?

Adam isn't sure he wants to do yardwork for Miss Winters. She lives in a run-down old house on an overgrown lot, doesn't want him knocking on the door, and warns him to stay out of the fenced-in backyard. And now a strange man in a black suit calls her the Spider Lady! Something creepy is going on here.

But Adam needs the money, thanks to his stepsister Belinda's latest successful attempt to get him into trouble. And working with his new friend, Pelican, will be fun. But before Adam even realizes how it happened, he's become something of a spider himself—spinning a web of half-truths and misunderstandings that make Belinda even angrier and may cost him Pelican's friendship.

Before the mystery is solved, Adam finds that he and Belinda aren't so different after all . . . and that God's forgiveness is something a Christian needs—and can count on—time and time again.

K. R. Hamilton lives with her husband and kids in Birmingham, Alabama. She has worked as a ranch hand, a lumberjack, a census taker, and an archeological surveyor, among other things. She's not likely to run out of things to write about.

Adam Straight to the Rescue

Ketchup on pancakes?

Adam has always wanted brothers and sisters . . . but this ready-made family isn't quite what he had in mind. Three-year-old Jory is cute enough, although his fascination with meat-eating dinosaurs can get out of hand. But ten-year-old Belinda is another story. How can Adam put up with a sister who calls his mother E. S. (short for Evil Stepmother), makes up stories just to scare him, and eats ketchup on everything?

"When we get back from our camping trip," his mom assures him, "it'll seem like we've been together forever." Adam's not so sure, although the two-day trip packs enough adventure to last most families a lifetime. And in spite of—or maybe because of—runaway cars, midnight animal visitors, and trips to the emergency room, Adam does some serious thinking and praying about what it means to be a brother. As he says, "I don't know why I argue with You, God. It's hard work. And besides, You always win!"

K.R. Hamilton lives with her husband and kids in Birmingham, Alabama. She has worked as a ranch hand, a lumberjack, a census taker, and an archeological surveyor, among other things. She's not likely to run out of things to write about.